PENGUIN MODERN CLASSICS

Of the Farm

JOHN UPDIKE was born in 1932, in Shillington, Pennsylvania. He graduated from Harvard College in 1954, and spent a year in Oxford, England, at the Ruskin School of Drawing and Fine Art. From 1955 to 1957 he was a member of the staff of *The New Yorker*; since 1957 he has lived in Massachusetts. He is the author of twenty-one novels as well as numerous collections of short stories, poems and criticism. His novels have won the Pulitzer Prize, the National Book Award, the American Book Award, the National Book Critics Circle Award, the Rosenthal Award and the Howells Medal.

D1188069

John Updike

OF THE FARM

PENGUIN BOOKS

PENGUIN CLASSICS

Published by the Penguin Group
Penguin Books Ltd, 80 Strand, London WC2R ORL, England
Penguin Group (USA) Inc., 375 Hudson Street, New York, New York 10014, USA
Penguin Group (Canada), 90 Eglinton Avenue East, Suite 700, Toronto, Ontario, Canada M4P 2Y3
(a division of Pearson Penguin Canada Inc.)
Penguin Ireland, 25 St Stephen's Green, Dublin 2, Ireland (a division of Penguin Books Ltd)
Penguin Group (Australia), 250 Camberwell Road, Camberwell, Victoria 3124, Australia
(a division of Pearson Australia Group Pty Ltd)
Penguin Books India Pvt Ltd, 11 Community Centre, Panchsheel Park,
New Delhi – 110 017, India
Penguin Group (NZ), 67 Apollo Drive, Rosedale, North Shore 0632, New Zealand
(a division of Pearson New Zealand Ltd)
Penguin Books (South Africa) (Pty) Ltd, 24 Sturdee Avenue, Rosebank, Johannesburg 2196,
South Africa

Penguin Books Ltd, Registered Offices: 80 Strand, London WC2R ORL, England

www.penguin.com

First published 1965
First published in Great Britain by Hamish Hamilton 1968
This edition first published 1993
Published in Penguin Classics 2007
1

Of the Farm is a work of fiction. Names, characters, places and incidents are the products of the
author's imagination or are used fictitiously. Any resemblance to actual events, locales or
persons, living or dead, is entirely coincidental.

Printed in England by Clays Ltd, St Ives plc

978-0-141-18902-4

Consequently, when, in all honesty, I've recognized that man is a being in whom existence precedes essence, that he is a free being who, in various circumstances, can want only his freedom, I have at the same time recognized that I can want only the freedom of others.

—SARTRE

OF THE FARM

WE TURNED OFF the Turnpike onto a macadam highway, then off the macadam onto a pink dirt road. We went up a sharp little rise and there, on the level crest where Schoel-kopf's weathered mailbox stood knee-deep in honeysuckle and poison ivy, its flopped lid like a hat being tipped, my wife first saw the farm. Apprehensively she leaned forward beside me and her son's elbow heavily touched my shoulder from be-hind. The familiar buildings waited on the far rise, across the concave green meadow. "That's our barn," I said. "My mother finally had them tear down a big overhang for hay she always thought was ugly. The house is beyond. The meadow is ours. Schoelkopf's land ends with this line of sumacs." We rattled down the slope of road, eroded to its bones of sandstone, that ushered in our land.

"You own on both sides of the road?" Richard asked. He was eleven, and rather precise and aggressive in speech.

"Oh sure," I said. "Originally Schoelkopf's farm was part of ours, but my grandfather sold it off before moving to Olinger. Something like forty acres."

"How many did that leave?"

"Eighty. As far as you can see now, it belongs to the farm. It's probably the biggest piece of open land left this close to Alton."

"You have no livestock," Richard said. Though I had told him there was none, his tone was accusatory.

"Just some dogs," I said, "and a barn full of swallows, and

lots of woodchucks. My mother used to keep chickens before my father died."

"What's the point," Richard asked, "of a farm nobody farms?"

"You'll have to ask my mother." He was silent a moment, as if I had rebuked him—I had not meant to. I added, "I never understood it myself. I was your age when we moved here. No, I was older. I was fourteen. I've always felt young for my age."

Then he asked, "Whose woods are all these?" and I knew he knew my answer and meant me to give it proudly.

"Ours," I said. "Except for the right-of-way we sold the power line twenty years ago. They cut down everything and never used it. There, you can see the cut, that strip of younger trees. It's all grown up again. They cut down oaks and it came up maples and sassafras."

"What's the point," he asked, "of a right-of-way nobody uses right away?" He laughed clumsily and I was touched, for he was making a joke on himself, trying to imitate, perhaps, my manner, and to unlearn the precocious solemnity his fatherless years had forced on him.

"That's how things are down here," I said. "Sloppy. You're lucky to live in New York, where space is tight."

Peggy spoke. "It *does* seem like a lot of everything," she said, of the farm skimming around us, and brushed back her hair from her forehead and cheeks, a gesture she uses after any remark that might meet opposition, as a man would push back his sleeves.

It was true—whenever I returned, after no matter how great a gap of time, to this land, the acres flowed outward from me like a form of boasting. My wife had sensed this and was so newly my wife she thought it worth correcting. This instinct of correction in her was precious to me (my first wife, Joan, had never criticized me at all, which itself seemed a deadly kind of criticism) but I dreaded its encounter with my mother.

Joan in her innocence had once gently suggested that my mother needed a washing machine. She had never been forgiven. My instinct, now, in these last moments before my mother was upon us, was to talk about her aloud, as if to expel what later must be left unsaid.

"Richard," I said, "there *is* a tractor. It drags a rotating cutter bar behind it that cuts the hay. It's the law in Pennsylvania that if your farm is in soil bank you must cut your weeds twice a summer."

"What's soil bank?"

"I don't know exactly. Farms that aren't farmed."

"Who drives the tractor?"

"My mother."

"It'll kill her," Peggy said harshly.

"She knows it," I said, as harshly.

Richard asked, "Can I drive it?"

"I wouldn't think so. Children do it around here, but they get"—I rejected the word "mangled"; a contemporary of mine had had his pelvis broken, and I envisioned his strange swirling limp—"hurt once in a while."

I expected him to insist, but he was distracted. "What's *that*?" The pink ruin had flashed by in the smothering greenery.

"That's the foundation of the old tobacco shed."

"You could put a roof on it and have a garage."

"It burned down forty years ago, when somebody else owned the farm."

Peggy said, "Before your mother bought it back?"

"Don't put it like that. She thinks now that my father wanted to buy it back too."

"Joey, I'm frightened!"

Her exclamation coincided with the blind moment when I negotiated the upward twist in the road that carried us around the barn. A car hurtling down the road heedlessly would be hidden long enough to produce a collision. But in the thousands of times I had risked it, it had never happened, though the young locals out in their jalopies liked to speed along our stretch, to tease the dogs and to annoy my mother. At night they sometimes roamed the fields in pick-up trucks, spotting deer with their headlights. It was dusk now. I pulled safely around the barn, parked on its ramp, which was grassy with disuse, and told Peggy, "Don't be. I don't expect you and she to get along. I thought she would with Joan but she didn't."

"And she has less reason to like me."

"Don't think that. Just be yourself. I love you."

But the declaration was given hastily, with a jerky pat of her thigh, for already my mother's shape, a solid blur, had emerged from the house and was moving through the blue shadow of the hemlock that guarded the walk. It was this tree that brought evening into the house early; many times at this hour as a boy I had been surprised, looking out of the window, thinking night had arrived, to see sunlight like raw ore still heaped on the upper half of the barn wall. With a guilty quickness I opened the car door and waved and hailed my mother: "Hi-i!"

"Pilgrims!" she called back, a faint irony barely audible in the strange acoustics of the engine's silence, as our Citroën hissingly settled through its cushions of air.

I was shocked by how slowly she moved along the walk. I had seen her outrace my father from the barn to the house in the rain. She suffered from angina and, though she had never smoked, emphysema. The great effort of her life had been to purchase this farm and move us all to it, but her lungs, the doctor told her, were those of a hardened city-dweller. Against the August damp she wore a man's wool sweater, my grandfather's, gray and ribbed and buttoned down the front, over an old pink blouse I associated with childhood Easters. The collie pup, the only dog not in the pen, kept dashing at us, barking and bristling a few feet from the piscine face of the Citroën, and then racing back to my mother. He nipped at her agonizing slowness of step; the pallor of his throat and tail-tip scudded in the gloom of the lawn. The lawn was tall with plantain and sadly needed cutting.

While Richard and I took the suitcases from the trunk, Peggy nervously hurried down the walk to meet my mother halfway, irritating her, I feared, with this unconscious display of quick health. The even spacing of the sandstones under her high heels made her seem unstable. I seemed to see her with my mother's eyes, as a tall and painted woman toppling toward me, and simultaneously with my own, from the rear, as a retreating white skirt whose glimmering breadth was the center, the seat, of my life. Not fat, my wife, as a woman, is wide, with sloping swinging shoulders and a pelvic amplitude that affects me as a kind of radiance and that gives her stride a heartening openness, a sense of space between her thighs.

The two women kissed. They had met once before, at the wedding I had urged my mother not to attend. It had been held, a week after my divorce from Joan became final, in the downtown private chambers of a municipal judge whose son I knew. The building was a survival, with cage elevators and brown linoleum halls lined with office doors whose frosted glass suggested a row of lavatories. It had been June, hot. The windows were old-fashionedly flung open and the sounds of the East River lifted into the room. The judicial sanctum was capacious along obsolete lines of office space, and the furniture, which included a wooden bench where my mother sat, looked sparse and stray, as if these inanimate survivors of a vanished courthouse era had been humanly subjected to the bewildering thinning of mortality. My mother kept folding and unfolding and smoothing on her lap a tiny linen handkerchief which she would now and then, as if stung, dartingly press to the side of her neck. I had thought of her as being hopelessly out of place at this ceremony, but we were all displaced: my bride's virtually adolescent son; the stiffish Park Avenue couple of whom the wall-eyed wife was Peggy's maid of honor; the freckled ex-Olympic skier and ex-lover of Joan's and professional colleague of mine who was, for want of a better, best man; Peggy's father, a pink-faced widower who managed an Omaha department store; and, least expected, my hyperthyroid nephew-in-law, a Union Theological School student present as a kind of delegate from Joan and my children, who were in retreat with her parents beside a Canadian lake. In this weird congregation my mother was no embarrassment. The judge, a gentle old shark in a seersucker suit, was charming to her. As if filing a bulky brief, with burled brown hands that he held in the bent-fingered manner of a manual workman, he carefully seated her on the bench. There she patted herself and panted in rapid faint eddies, like a resting dog. Her coming here (by bus, with an hour's wait in Philadelphia), which I had resisted, now seemed an extravagant exertion on my behalf, and I was grateful. I was conscious of her presence even at the pinnacle of the rite, when in the corner of my eye I saw Peggy's firm chin redden and the dark star of her lashes alter position as her profile lowered toward the shuddering bouquet of violets clasped at her waist. She had read that a bride previously married carried flowers not white and had spent the morning phoning around the city for violets in June. I felt her then, my bride, for all the demure youth of her profile, as middle-aged—felt us both to be standing, in vulnerable poses of beginning, on the verge of some great middle, beside a river grander than its shores. Seen through the flung-open window beyond the judge's robed shoulder, the river, tilted by our height, supported a slow traffic of miniature barges and, elevating through the tall afternoon in which Brooklyn was a glistening vision stitched with derricks, tipped into this room a breeze that nudged a few papers on the legally impassive oak desk. A single fly circled a knotted light cord. Then the vows were sworn and I had a sense of falling, of collapsing, at last, into the firm depths of a deed too long and too painfully suspended above completion. Turning to receive congratulations, to bestow and accept kisses from the few who had climbed to this height with me, I was confused to discover that my mother's eyes were remote with anger and her cheek, for all the heat of the day, was cool.

———

Now IN COOL AIR I kissed her and her face felt feverish. Fall, which comes earlier inland, was present not so much as the scent of fallen fruit in the orchard as a lavender tinge in the dusk, a sense of expiration. The meadow wore a strip of mist where a little rivulet, hardly a creek, choked by weeds and watercress, trickled and breathed. A bat like a speck of pain jerked this way and that in the membranous violet between the treetops. My mother had touched Peggy quickly and as if for contrast her hands lingered on me—one on my forearm, the other on my shoulder. "How tired are you?" she asked. She meant that I looked tired.

"Not at all," I said. "We beat the rush across the bridge and had a hamburger in New Jersey."

"Oh I didn't *mean*," my mother said, turning too adroitly, "that *Peggy* looked tired. I've never seen Peggy look anything but cheerful." Her voice seemed generated forward in her body, in her throat and mouth rather than in her lungs, and, disassociated from the depths of her person, was breathy but more agile than ever. There was something ironical in this agility, and in the way she held her shoulders cupped, as if to deepen her lungs—a kind of parody, perhaps, designed to distract us from her unexaggerated condition.

Peggy's cheerful expression faded; then she gamely grinned and said, "It's just a front."

"A delightful one," my mother said.

I took Peggy's arm to lead her toward the house, but she

moved away from me, to admit Richard, who had come up behind us. I had forgotten him. He had insisted on lugging the heavier suitcase, which held his mother's clothes. He shifted it to his left hand and held out his right for my mother to shake. "You have quite a farm here, Mrs. Robinson," he said. He could deepen his voice impressively, for short utterances.

"Why, I thank you, kind sir," my mother said. "You've hardly seen any of it. I was hoping your parents could get here early enough for us to take a walk in the light."

"We can do that tomorrow," Peggy said. "I'd love it."

"I have to mow the fields," I said, wondering if only I had flinched at my mother's imprecise use of the word "parents."

She said, "Poor Joey. So conscientious."

"I like what I've seen," Richard assured her. His voice relaxed into a childish register. "We passed an old foundation you could very easily make into a two-car garage."

"The old tobacco shed," I explained. "I always thought that would be the pro shop when we made the farm into a golf course." The golf course was a family joke, conceived when my father was living, whose exact quality I had never understood; but I inserted it here as a shield for my stepson's innocence.

My mother studied him, feigned dismay, and cried, "But that's where the best blackberries grow!"

We all laughed in gratitude at her relieving, if only for a moment, the darkness that had come upon her since her health had weakened. Her spirit had acquired a troubling resonance, a murky subtlety doubly oppressive out of doors—as if in being surrounded by her farm we had been plunged into the very territory of her thoughts.

Walking with that perhaps ironical slowness, my mother led us into the house. Since my first return from college nearly twenty years ago, my homecomings had tapered to the moment that now again was upon me; my feet touched the abrasive sandstone sill of our back porch while the dogs with joyful savagery yapped in the pen next to the crippled privet bush once gored by a runaway bull that my grandmother had tamed with an apron. It had happened the first summer we lived on the farm. A Mennonite dairy farmer rented our meadow for a small herd that included this rust-colored bull, who had found a slack section of the fence behind the spring-house. He pranced up into our yard, snorted, attacked the little round bright green bush, and stood there shaking his head as if to silence a buzzing in his ears. Flapping the apron and speaking to him with the same cross sibilance she employed to hold door-to-door salesmen at bay, my grandmother—the rest of us cowering and shouting in the kitchen—protected the bit of privet, a transplant from her beloved Olinger yard, until the Mennonite's hired hands arrived with ropes. The bush had lived, but each winter's burden of snow had spread its split wider, even as it grew taller.

We entered the kitchen. Its warm worn wood was softly lit. We had never, all the time I was growing up, owned enough lamps, or bought strong enough bulbs. We were thrifty in small things and spendthrift in large. The interior of the thick-walled little house had been strangely enriched, gaudily barnacled, by gifts I had sent over the years. Christmases, birthdays, anniversaries, even Mother's Days had deposited upon the windowsills and cupboard shelves trinkets of Danish pewter and Mexican pottery and Italian glass mailed by me, usually in haste and late, from Cambridge and Rome and Berkeley and New York. I felt these gifts, however expensive, to have been cheap substitutes for my love and my presence, and it was as if, entering the remembered interior expecting to find my threadbare youth, I found instead these gaudy scraps of my maturity. Each time I returned I more strongly resented how much of myself was already here. Pictures of me—of me graduating (three times), of me getting married (the first time), of me clowning in the sun with my children, of me staring mummified from the head of a yellowed news clipping "permanized" in plastic—were propped and hung throughout the living room, along with various medals and certificates I had won as a schoolboy; I was so abundantly memorialized it seemed I must be dead. Whereas my father, who hated to have his picture taken (for thirty years the yearbooks of the high school where he taught had printed the same unflattering photograph of him), was nowhere in sight, which gave his absence vitality. I could see him shying out of camera range, saying, "Keep my ugly mug out of it." I listened for his footstep to scuff on the porch and for his hand to wrench open the back door with that strange vehemence he had, as if meeting more than halfway the possibility of its being locked. It did not seem incredible that he would walk into the living room holding his evening gift, a dewy pint box of tricolor ice cream, and look at me with his mixture of mischief and sorrow, and shake my hand and turn to my mother and say, "The kid looks healthy," and turn to my wife and say, "You must be feeding him right."

But he did not; the four of us were alone. There was another absence on the walls. Above the sofa whose pillows were fuzzed with shed dog hair, there had hung for twelve years a formal portrait of Joan, a companion to a photograph of me taken at the same time, in an Alton studio, when we were both in our early twenties and newly married. My mother had made the appointment without consulting us, and we had both resented it. I had thought such sentimentality uncharacteristic of my mother. I still saw her with the eyes of her child, as someone whose presence was renewed each day. Her passion for mementos of me had begun before I realized that I had truly left. Obediently we had climbed into the car one hot noon and drove ten miles south to keep the appointment. Joan had worn, as if to express simultaneously her contempt for this business and her confidence in her young beauty, a simple cotton dress, a dress that a farm girl might have peddled strawberries in, with a faded pattern of small blue flowers on a yellow ground and a broad square neckline that carelessly displayed her well-turned throat and shoulders. When the proofs came back, my mother chose for enlargement one that had caught Joan off guard, in one of those apprehensive moments, frequent with her, when her body like that of a flower toward light seemed to elongate in response to some distant challenge. She was shown from the hips up, kneeling with a concealed knee on the seat of a chair whose curved backrest her hands gripped with an intensity that accented their fine bones. She had had finer hands than Peggy. A pale, rounded, fully extended right arm held her posture erect and her face turned three-quarters toward an upward light that all but dissolved the suggestion of a pout on her lips. Through the stiffness of the pose and the softness of the focus there yet had penetrated the keenness of her grace, a natural grace rendered elusive by her air of reservation, her stubborn shyness, which in turn would be dazzlingly contradicted, slashed through, by one of her brilliant and absolutely symmetrical smiles. The picture held a secret. Joan had been pregnant. Seven months later, Ann, our elder daughter, had been born. And this immanence mingled with the cherished picture my memory had held behind the posed picture, of Joan grudgingly shrugging herself into the yellow dress and of the stifling midday ride into downtown Alton, so typical of those strained early visits to the farm, when the dust hung as rose-colored mist after the passage of each car, and my father would bring home ice cream from his daily tussle with his students, and my boyish loyalties fluttered bewildered between my mother and my wife, between whom, unaccountably, there was disharmony. It was typical of their relations that the photograph turned out to be not what my mother really wanted. "I had wanted," she told Joan years later, "a picture of your smile."

In its place above the sofa, not quite filling the telltale rectangle of less discolored wallpaper, there had been substituted an idyllic little landscape, a much-reduced print of an oil, that had ornamented my room as a child, when we lived in my grandparents' house in the town. Instantly—and I wanted my mother to see me doing this, as a kind of rebuke—I went to examine the print closely. The pentagonal side of a barn was diagonally bisected by a purple shadow cast by nothing visible, and a leafless tree of uncertain species stood rooted in lush grass impossibly green. Beyond, I revisited, bending deeper into the picture, a marvellous sky of lateral stripes of pastel color where as a child I had imagined myself treading, upside-down, a terrain of crayons. The tiny black V of one flying bird was planted in this sky, between two furrows of color, so that I had imagined that if my fingers could get through the glass they could pluck it up, like a carrot sprout. This quaint picture, windowing a fabulous rural world, had hung, after we had moved to the farmhouse, in the room at the head of the stairs, where I had slept as an adolescent and where, when I had gone away, my father had slept in turn. Climbing the stairs with Richard, I feared I would find my father there, asleep under the glaring light, a slippery magazine spread on his chest and his spectacles shielding his closed eyes. Instead I discovered, tucking Richard into the empty bed, that my mother had not hidden the photograph of Joan, but merely switched it with the landscape. Joan hung on my old wall.

"Who's the attractive girl?" Richard asked. When my voice moved to tell him, it met an impenetrable obstacle, as if his not knowing by sight the woman his mother had replaced were a precious piece of ignorance it was my duty to preserve. I pushed his large furry head, bushy with a crew-cut that needed renewing, against my chest so he would not see my face. When he saw it anyway, I shakily explained, "This house is too full of me."

———

BEFORE I PUT RICHARD to bed, we had eaten and talked. My mother, not knowing if we would eat on the road or not, had prepared a Pennsylvania snack, a meal by our standards: pork sausage, pepper cabbage (remembering a fondness I had forgotten, she had saved for me, as a treat, the cold-looking, hot-tasting scraped cabbage heart), applesauce, shoo-fly pie, the caffeine-less coffee her heart could tolerate. Peggy and Richard were rather overwhelmed by this brown, steaming outlay. I was surprised to see the boy, at an age when I never had had enough shoo-fly pie, politely refuse a second piece. My mother offered him coffee and Peggy said that he never drank it.

"Never?"

"Last summer with my father," Richard said, "on a camping trip to the Adirondacks, we drank it, because the condensed milk was unbearable."

"Yes, and you came home sick," Peggy said.

"It's caffeine-free," my mother said, and poured him half a cup. The act of pouring, in comfortable association with the shape and grain of our old dining table, led her to talk; we had always talked, when there had been a family, around food. "I think I began drinking coffee," she said, "when I was three. I remember sitting in the high chair, right where you're sitting, Peggy, and having a big black cup set on the tray in front of me. I don't know what my mother was thinking of, except in those days nobody knew anything about nutrition, and my dad never had milk in the house. He drank a dozen cups a day to the day he died, black, as black as possible, and hotter than any man I ever knew. Right off the stove, he'd swig it down; he was very proud of this ability. It was the sort of thing, Richard, that people used to be proud of."

Richard put his fingers on the cup and, as if the contact put him in direct touch with my mother, said boldly, "Tell me, Mrs. Robinson, about your farm."

"What would you like to know about it? I'm sure that Joey"—she paused, finding this name for me strange when spoken to my stepson, yet no more able than I to think of any other—"has told you already more than you want to know." She looked at me quickly and went on, "Or maybe he hasn't. He probably never talks about the farm. It's always depressed him."

"Your father," Richard said, "the man who could drink the coffee so hot—did he sell it, or what? I can't quite fit the elements together."

My mother folded her arms on the table and leaned forward, a solicitous-appearing gesture developed to soothe her breathing. "My father," she said, "was like my son—the farm depressed him. *His* father had made him work too hard on it, and when he was"—she studied me, still searching for my name—"about the age my son is now, he sold it, and moved us all to the town where *he*"—she pointed at me—"grew up."

"What did your father do for a living then?" Richard asked.

"Well, that's it. He didn't do anything. He was a man without a vocation, and if you don't have a vocation the next best thing is to have a farm. He sat in a chair and drank coffee and watched his money go down the drain in the stock market crash."

"My father says there will never be another stock market crash."

"Well, I hope not, but like a lot of unfortunate things it probably had its purpose. It improved my dad's manners, I know, because as long as he had any money he was a pretty ugly customer."

"Richard," Peggy said, "is very fond of his father." She smoothed back her hair. Her remark seemed misjudged to me; she had felt an insinuation in my mother's words that was not there. My mother had loved her father, and thought that "ugliness" was a rather desirable human attribute. It seemed dense of Peggy not to feel this, and I confess that the way she invariably, in Richard's presence, rose to defend the man she had divorced five years ago irritated me, as does any response that has degenerated into a reflex. Yet I sympathized with her nervousness, for my mother has a dangerous way of treating children as equals. Years ago, in this kitchen, my son Charlie, who was then two, while parading around the table with a yardstick, accidentally tapped my mother with it. Without a moment's hesitation she pulled it from his hands and smartly smacked him back. As Joan comforted him, my mother, still holding the yardstick—an orange one stamped with the name of an Alton hardware store—explained that the boy had been "giving her the eye" all morning, and for some time had been planning to "put her to the test." As primitive worshippers invest the indifferent universe with pointed intentions, so my mother read into the animate world, including infants and dogs, a richness of motive that could hardly be there— though, like believers everywhere, she had a way of making her environment supply corroboration.

"Good for Richard," she said levelly, and tipped back her head to give Peggy the benefit of the reading half of her bifocals. "And why shouldn't he be?"

I flinched, guessing that Peggy would make an answer; but Richard, whose eyes had the shininess of the enchanted— the frogs and deer who are really princes—luckily insisted that my mother's tale continue. "How did you buy back the farm without any money?"

"We sold the house," my mother said, "the house in town where *he*"—me—"was born. After the war. You see, Richard, after the Depression, when everybody lost their money, except for Bing Crosby, there was a war, when everybody, even schoolteachers, made some, if they weren't killed."

"Who was Bing Crosby?"

"A very popular singer. That was a joke."

"I see," he said, and solemnly smiled. He has the gap between his front teeth that usually goes with freckles, of which he has none, having inherited from his father a smooth and sanguine skin.

"The war was over, and my husband and I had a little saved—he had worked summers and I had been, can you imagine, a parachute cutter—and the farm came onto the market. I went to the old fella who used to give me advice when I asked for it. Before I had Joey, I asked him if I should, because it was supposed to be dangerous for me, and he said, 'It's dead blood that doesn't flow.' By this he meant, I thought, that a line of blood, a family, must have a child or it is dead. So I had my son, and none of my aunts could believe I could have been so clever. They'd thought I was a freak. Now I wanted my farm, and he told me, 'There's a Spanish proverb, "Take what you want, and pay the price." ' And that's what I did."

There was a silence as we estimated the price. Richard asked, "Did your husband like farming?"

No was shouted in me so loud I said, to hush it, "He never farmed."

"He never farmed," my mother said. "That's right. But he bought me a tractor and let me keep the fields mowed. He was a city boy, like you are."

"What's the point," Richard asked, as I had told him to, "of a farm nobody farms?"

I feared we had gone beyond hushing, but my mother unexpectedly seemed pleased with the question, and moved her head still farther forward above her folded arms, to give herself breath for a full answer. "Why," she said rapidly, "I guess that's the point, that nobody farms it. Land is like people, it needs a rest. Land is *just* like a person, except that it never dies, it just gets very tired."

"Furthermore," I told Richard, to relieve her laboring voice, "we do farm it somewhat. Sometimes we have the hay baled and sell it. A few years ago we let an Amishman rent the upper field to plant it with corn; we ourselves used to grow vegetables and sell strawberries."

"Yes," my mother said, abruptly speaking to Peggy, "we used to make this sophisticated young Harvard man and his refined wife from Boston go out along the road with a board and two trestles and peddle berries to the Sunday traffic!" It startled me to hear how Joan and my earlier self had become part of my mother's saga of the farm.

"We didn't mind," I said, as if to make myself less a myth, and less removed from the wife who had not sold strawberries.

"You used to hate it," my mother said positively. "You used to be so afraid nobody would stop." She explained to Peggy, "He doesn't eat strawberries so he couldn't understand why anybody would want them."

"He eats strawberries now," Peggy told her.

My mother asked me, "Do you?"

"On ice cream," I said.

"Who was the old fella?" Richard asked.

My mother blinked. "Old fella?"

"The old fella you asked advice from whenever you wanted to do anything."

"Oh—that's a story maybe you shouldn't know. What do you think, Peggy?"

"I don't know the story."

"He was an old cousin, Richard, named Uncle Rupe, that some people thought had been very partial to my mother. And stayed too long after his attentions were appropriate, some said. Anyway, I was his pet, so there must have been something strange. He was the only person who ever thought I was cute."

"That seems surprising," Richard said.

My mother stared; but the boy's bright-eyed and flatly fascinated face, quite bare of any impudent intention, was a sufficient shield. She stated, "That's what *I* thought, too."

Peggy had stiffened in the moment of danger and now said, "Richard, it's an hour past your bedtime."

"I'm not sleepy," he said. "It must be the change of climate. Maybe it's a matter of altitude. The men who climbed Everest couldn't sleep hardly at all."

I asked my mother, "Have you thrown out those old science-fiction anthologies of mine? Richard is just starting to read science fiction."

"It's deliciously frightening," he said.

"Nothing's been moved," my mother told me, in a weary voice that harbored an irrelevant note of complaint.

I went to the shelves, where as many books were horizontal as upright, below the window that looked toward the barn, which was now a pale hollow in the night, eclipsing stars; and there, under some paperback Thorne Smith and P. G. Wodehouse that had long ago amused me and that now, in the very look of their peeling and outmoded covers, revived the dusty pollen-stuffed sensations of those interminable summer days before I acquired a driver's license and could escape the farm, the fat faded science-fiction collection Doubleday had printed in the Forties was preserved: a miracle. Time's battering had bleached not only the spine but the margin of the front cover not covered by another book. With this frayed bribe I urged Richard up the narrow stairs. "Brush your teeth," Peggy called after us. I left him tucked in, his kiss tasting of Crest, propped up on two pillows beneath the old bridge lamp with the dented paper shade that my father used to sleep directly under while it burned. The lamp had been standing cobwebbed in a corner, unplugged.

Downstairs, the women were doing the dishes. With my fresh vision of Joan's photograph, I remembered how she had chronically offended my mother by too diligently helping her. My mother was fearfully sensitive to any suggestion that she was being ousted, perhaps because her own mother, who had held command of the kitchen until her death at seventy-nine, had fiercely resisted ouster by her. Peggy had seized the dominant position at the sink while my mother docilely fetched and stacked. The docility was not merely an optical impression; there was no hint in my mother's atmosphere—a volatile pressure system to which I am more sensitive than to weather itself—of a latent storm of resentment, and I was struck again by how weak she had become. She carried dishes to Peggy with the wary explorative motions of an invalid. I helped her. The dishes done, she slowly gathered three wine glasses and the bottle of sherry that was the only liquor in the house, and a cellophane bag of pretzels, and we went into the living room and talked.

TALK—it seemed throughout my growing-up that there was no end of talk. Talk was everything to us—food and love, money and mud, God and the Devil, confession, philosophy, and exercise. And though my grandfather's sculpturally spaced utterances, given additional dignity and point by many judicious throat-clearings and heavenward gesticulations of his dry-skinned hands, had ceased, and my father's humorous prancing whine had fallen silent forever, yet my mother's voice alone, rising and falling, sighing itself away and wishing itself reborn, letting itself grow so slack and diffuse it seemed the murmur of nature and then abruptly narrowing into swift self-justification, managed, for all the distention of her heart and lungs, to maintain almost uninterrupted the dense vocal outpouring in which I had been bathed and raised. Talk in our house was a continuum sensitive at all points of past and present and tirelessly harking back and readjusting itself, as if seeking some state of equilibrium finally free of irritation. My mother was bothered by my saying, an hour back, of my father, "He never farmed," and implying, with this, that the

farm had been a burden upon him and had shortened his life.
I felt this was true; my mother feared it might be. Her method
of expiation, of seeking equilibrium, was to describe to Peggy,
in ample and convoluted and cute detail, our financial and
personal situation when we made the move. In this story, which
slightly changed each time I heard it, her mother ("who," my
mother said to Peggy, "reminds me a lot of you; she didn't
have red hair, but she had your energy, and your way with the
dishes, and your pointed nose. If I had inherited my mother's
nose instead of my father's shapeless blob I wouldn't have
wound up as a crazy old hermit") was finding the Olinger
house too big to run. My grandfather was settling into apathy.
The heating and maintenance bills were driving my father to
an early grave. I, my mother's son, was in danger of becoming
"an Olinger know-nothing, a type of humanity, Peggy, that
must be seen to be believed—you can't believe it, but the people of that town with absolute seriousness consider it the center of the universe. They don't want to *go* anywhere, they
don't want to *know* anything, they don't want to *do* anything
except sit and admire each other. I didn't want my only child
to be an Olingerite; I wanted him to be a *man*." So she had
brought me here. And my father; well—"My husband and I,
Peggy, never had much imagination, and we had very simple
needs, so whenever one of us managed to think of something
he or she really wanted, the other would try to help. I've
really wanted only two—no, three—things in my life. The
first thing I wanted was a horse, and my father got it for me,
and then I couldn't keep it when we moved away. The next
two things I really wanted were my son and my farm, and
George let me have both."

Peggy asked, "And what did he want?"

My mother tipped her head, as if to identify a remote
bird-call.

The question was very clear in Peggy's mind and she tried
to share this clarity. "What did you help him get? He gave

you Joey and the farm; what did you give him?" Her expression was polite, but her eyes, whose lids showed green shadow lingering from the city, were dangerously tired.

My heart was thudding; my tingling fingers felt swollen around the cold core of the wine-glass stem. My mother's silences, in which her soul plunged backwards from her eyes and mouth and revisited the darkness in which I might have remained unborn, were as terrible as ever.

"Why," she said at last, expansively spreading her hands, "his freedom!"

In this reply, this daring vindication of her marriage, all her old wit sprang to life; and it dismayed me to see that Peggy was puzzled. Her chin went stubborn and I felt her resisting, as she would resist the fit of a dress handed down to her from another, the frame of assumptions and tolerances in which my mother's description of my father's anguished restlessness as "his freedom" was beautifully congruous. My mother within the mythology she had made of her life was like a mathematician who, having decreed certain severely limited assumptions, performs feats of warping and circumvention and paradoxical linkage that an outside observer, unrestricted to the plane of their logic, would find irksomely arbitrary. And, with the death of my father and my divorce of Joan, there was no inside observer left but myself—myself, and the adoring dogs.

Peggy brutally asked, "Can you give a person freedom?" I saw that my mother's describing as a gift her failure to possess my father had angered her; it had touched the sore point within her around which revolved her own mythology, of women giving themselves to men, of men in return giving women a reason to live.

My mother chose to understand her in terms of another religion. "I suppose," she said, "only *God* really gives. But people can give by not denying, which comes to the same thing." And then, like a stream swirling past a snag, the flow of her talk resumed, and her memories of buying the farm broadened to the farm itself, as it had been at the moment of purchase, ravaged, eroded; as it had been in her girlhood, the big upper field an ocean of barley, the little flat upper field laid out in tomato rows, the triangular field across from the meadow golden-green with sweet corn, the far field silver-green with alfalfa, a truck garden of potatoes and onions and cabbage and staked peas stretched all along the sandy ridge beyond the orchard whose overburdened lower limbs wore crutches, and even the woods fruitful, of berries and hickory nuts and firewood; the farm as it was now, at rest, the shaggy fields needing to be mowed. Thus her talk at last reached solid matter: the purpose of this trip was for me to run the tractor, which she had grown too frail to do. The Commonwealth would fine her if it wasn't done. Our visit had been arranged in several gingerly phone calls in which my mother and I, our pauses shadowed by a crosshatch of conversations in New Jersey, had guessed at what the other wanted—I was to mow and she was to meet Peggy, to deepen her acquaintance with my wife, to learn, if possible, to love her. Peggy was asleep. My wide-hipped, heavy-lidded wife had been carried off during my mother's discourse. She lay unconscious in the faded embrace of our old maroon wing chair, once my grandfather's favorite forum. Her pointed yellow high-heeled shoes lay beside her feet as if dislodged by a sudden shift of momentum. Her feet, whose long toes were gauzily masked by the ashen nylon of her stockings, rested sideways on the floor, dragged by the length of her legs, which were propped at the knees against one arm of the chair. Her twisted skirt revealed a dark curve of stocking-top. Her forearms, freckled and downy, one slack palm and veined inner wrist turned upward into lamplight, lay crossed in her lap, and her averted face leaned into the shadowed red cloth of the chair while her long hair, having broken the clasp of its pins, flowed motionless down the submissive curve of her back and across the white of her neck.

She overflowed the chair, and I felt proud before my mother, as if, while she was talking of the farm, I were silently displaying to her my own demesne seized from the world. Yet my mother's gaze, after lingering on the long female body curled asleep as trustfully as that of a child, returned to me offended. Before she could say anything that would wound us both, I impatiently asked, "Why can't we hire someone to mow? Why must you and I do it?"

"It's our place."

"It's your place."

"It will be yours soon enough."

"Don't say that."

"I mean it as a pleasant fact. Are you serious about the golf course?"

"Of course not. It takes thousands of dollars to make one green, and then who'd run it? I live in New York."

"I've been thinking, you could sell the small flat field off in half-acre lots, I guess my ghost could put up with that, and use the money to keep the rest intact. There's not a week somebody doesn't call and ask me to sell them a piece. The vultures are gathering."

"What do they offer?"

"Well that's it, next to nothing. Two hundred an acre. They must think I'm completely addled by now. A Philadelphia Jew offered twenty-five thousand and would have left me the house and orchard; that's the fairest offer I've heard. I bet I could have jacked him up to forty."

"You paid four."

She shrugged. "That was twenty years ago. There's more people now, and more money. It's not the homely county you grew up in. The money's come back. Which reminds me—Schoelkopf. He has a grandson now and thinks he wants the meadow."

"All of it?"

"Oh, sure. He even slyly suggested, you know, it would be a

kindness to *you* if I were to turn a little profit and stop accepting support from my son."

"Don't let that be a factor."

"Aah"—she drew her hand across the air as her father used to do, a gesture that when I was a child reminded me of that mysterious sentence in the Rubáiyát about the moving finger, having writ, moving on—"don't be too quick. You have two wives now, and I can run up a lot of medical bills for myself. Doc Graaf wants me in the hospital now."

"Truly? You seem a little short of breath, but otherwise—"

"I have what they used to call 'spells.' The last one, I was out on the far field with the dogs and I think they must have dragged me back—all I remember is crawling upstairs on all fours and taking all the pills I could find, one of each. When I woke up it was the same time the next day and Flossie had half chewed through the window sash above the bookcase. They still get up there and look for George to come home."

"You should have called me."

"You were on your honeymoon. Anyway, Joey. Your father and I had our differences but there was one thing we agreed on and that was we wanted to die cheap. It's hard now, you know. The doctors have these machines that can keep you going long enough to empty everybody's bank account."

"You can't reduce everything to money."

"What would you reduce it to? Sex?"

I blushed, and in the space of a breath she took pity, continuing, "Now tell me honestly. Am I a burden?"

"No. The money I send you is the least of my problems."

"I believe *that*—but his pension almost stretches and I can do without a little more. I don't want you to wind up hating me on account of a few dollars; we've come too far for that."

"It won't come to that. I'm all right, money, sex, everything."

"May I ask, now, how much *did* the divorce cost?"

"Well—for just the lawyers, not less than four thousand." The same amount, I realized, that the farm had cost.

"That's the lawyers. And Joan—?"

"Was very modest and considerate as usual. If she remarries in two years, the pinch should be bearable."

"With three young children that's quite an if. Joan doesn't have your new one's drive."

Grief, or impatience—I had lost the ability to tell them apart—strained my voice. "Mother, that's something I can't control."

She settled back contentedly. She was sitting in a chair that had always embarrassed me, a wire-mesh lawn chair that, invited by poverty, had come indoors, painted blue. "Now tell me. Don't be polite. Do you want me to sell?"

"The farm?"

"A piece of it. Some lots."

"Of course not."

"Why not?"

Because, the real reason was, she didn't want to. "Because it's not necessary."

"Will you promise me one thing? Will you tell me when it is?"

"I'd rather leave it up to you to guess."

"Better not. I'm not as good at guessing as I used to be."

So the appearance of a bargain was important to her. I said, "I promise."

Peggy stirred; her long legs shifted away from some ache, a foot tipped over an empty shoe that had been upright, an unconscious hand tugged her skirt down.

"Your bride," my mother said, "will have a stiff neck."

Peggy's eyes were open. She had heard this. She blinked, bewildered by where she was. Her drowsy state seemed to me a vulnerability. I stood, turning my back on my mother, and offered Peggy my hand. Weak with sleep, she tried to decipher my urgent, stern, beseeching hand, and then looked up to my face, where she must have read my conception of this moment as an emergency and a rescue, for she made an effort to collect herself. "Come on, lady," I said. "Let's get you into bed."

"How silly," she said, and put her hand in mine, and let me pull her up, and stood. In stocking feet she seemed small beside me. Her hands, her hands are slightly large and reddish in the knuckles and fingertips and always come to my imagination as oval in shape. I think I was first attracted to her, first noticed her at that first party, by the way she stood, awkward and grave, with her hands inert at her sides, incurved toward her thighs, like tools not being used; the full length of her arms was displayed, and there was a suggestion, in her refusal to shield her front with a held cigarette or a fending gesture, that she could be taken.

"Good night, Mrs. Robinson," she said. "Sorry to be so dopey."

"I think you're the only one of us with sense," my mother said. "Good night, Peggy. There's an extra blanket if you need it in the bureau." She did not wish me good night, as if I were certain to return.

In our room—my parents' old room, with a picture of me as a child on the wall—Peggy asked me, "What were you talking about?" In the picture my lips were lightly parted, my chin was pointed, my nose was straight and flat and saddled with freckles. My eyes, my eyes absorbed me, they were so sweetly clear, so completely clairvoyant, so unblaming. We seemed married in their sight. Beneath the picture stood the bedside table, supporting a lamp with a pleated plastic shade partially melted by accidental contact with the bulb, a peacock-blue runner, an iron ashtray shaped like an elephant. I visualized in the closed drawer bundled letters, snapshots, report cards, and painstaking checkbook stubs. On a shelf between the legs near the floor rested, neglected, heavy as a casket, the family Bible, leathery and ridged, edged in gold, inherited from my father's father's father. Once I had written my name on its genealogy page.

I answered Peggy, "The farm."

"What about it?"

"Whether we should sell any of it."

"What did you decide?"

"It had been decided already. She won't sell."

"Do you want her to?"

"Not much."

"Why not?"

"I don't know. I have no idea. This place has always given me hay fever."

"I thought you were going to say it gave you the creeps."

"That's what my father used to say."

My mother's voice, with that note of timidity that was more penetrating, from her, than a shout, called me from the foot of the stairs. I had taken off my shirt and put it on again before going down.

"The dogs," she said. "Could you take what's left of the sausage to them and set a pan of water on the straw? I hate to be a wheedler, but if it's me they'll think I've come to give them a run and to tell the truth I think I've overindulged."

"Do you feel funny?"

"Queerly, as Pop would have put it." I looked at her anxiously; she was standing in the living room, just back from the kitchen doorway, as if in a shallow box. A single dim bulb was burning in the kitchen, over by the stove, and her forehead had the metallic tint of my grandfather's skin in his last days. Her thick hair, whose dominant gray was mixed with residual black in a blend that tasted bitter to the eye, hung stiffly, a pyramidal mass, about her head. With her hair down she had seemed witchlike to me ever since as a child I would watch her brushing it in the Olinger back yard and pulling it from the brush so that birds might weave her shed strands into their nests; at night, when she brushed her hair in my parents' bedroom, from my bed I could see blue sparks leaping.

I asked, "Should you have any pills?" She moved a few

inches forward, and her shoulders seemed strangely creamy in the stronger light. One strap of her nightgown was awry.

"Oh, I have them. Pills in the icebox, pills under my pillow—" She changed her tone. "Don't worry yourself, just give the dogs their water and take your wife to bed. She may find the night chilly—the old Indian blanket is in the third drawer of Daddy's bureau. I'll be all right once I lie down."

"Should you sleep on the sofa?"

"I always do. I haven't slept hardly at all upstairs since he— went."

I tried to smile, and shrugged instead. With the abruptness of pain she turned her back on me. My father had died a summer ago.

I went out into the dark. The porch sandstone was warm and granular on my bare feet, and then the dew was cuttingly cold. The privet bush showed a split face to the moon. Far on my left an owl emitted its matronly exclamation of distaste or mourning, and farther still a trailer truck, with an exasperated hiss, shifted gears on the highway; both sounds came from the same direction, from the almost transparent strip of woods, ours, between our yard and the fields adjoining the road, once the Mennonite's dairy farm, now a budding housing development. It was among these trees that my mother all winter long scattered on cupping rocks and exposed stumps handfuls of sunflower seed for the birds. It was along this rim of woods that she felt the world's invasion pressing most.

The dogs seemed glad to see me, though they were fierce with strangers; there had been several biting incidents, and one lawsuit. It must have been that my mother and I smelled subtly alike to them. Or perhaps they sensed my father in me. They were, besides the collie pup—which my mother had taken from the Schoelkopfs rather than let them have him "put away"—two part-chow mongrels from the same litter, their mother's mother a dog I had known well, Mitzi, my dog, with her tongue spotted black like a pansy, and her shimmering bristling ruff of copper hair as fine as the poll of a dandelion, and her out-of-proportion small and emotional ears, and her dainty-boned hind legs that were severed, one July noon, by the cutter bar of a hired tractor driven by Schoelkopf's son, while I was off at college. It was after that accident—the dog had to be shot—that my mother bought our third-hand tractor, and learned to run it, and taught my father and me. Eerily silent, as if their pitch of expectation were higher than I could hear, the dogs thrashed against my legs. I set down the sausage platter, reserving in my hand a piece for the pup, which I threw down for him on a separate patch of straw, and took the empty pan, careful to latch the pen door behind me, back to the porch and pumped it full, thus becoming, myself, one more country noise. The rattling squeak of a pump handle will carry, on a warm open night, from farm to farm. Now the owl's monotone protest was overruled by a whippoorwill. I put the swaying pan (light leaped and slopped; dog-noses recklessly converged) back in the pen, examined the state of the moon, and guessed it to be one night short of full. I stood a moment in the open air feeling time flow, and almost gratefully returned to the closeness of the house.

I switched the remaining kitchen light off. In the living room my mother lay in the dark. I went in to her, though Peggy's waiting upstairs pulled on my skull. The invisible mementos and objects around me seemed expectant, like the votive rubbish left at a shrine. The smell was not of my youth but of dust. I sat in my grandmother's rocking chair, which tipped back abruptly under my weight, as if she had hopped out of the way. There was silence.

"The boy," my mother said, "seems bright."

"Yes, I think he is."

"It's interesting," she continued, "because the mother doesn't seem so."

This blow was delivered in the darkness like a pillow of warmth against my face. I felt myself at the point at which, years ago, in this same room, I had failed Joan. Yet I respected—was captive within—my mother's sense of truth. My response was weak. "Not?"

"I'm surprised at you," my mother went on, in a voice whose timbre was deadened by her horizontal position.

"At what?"

"That you would need a stupid woman to give you confidence."

"You don't know anything about her. You don't want to know."

"I know what I can't help knowing. I look at my son and see a man his father wouldn't recognize."

"You let him see for himself. You listen to me." I was whispering, hissing; I stood up, and the rocker, released, returned forward and struck the backs of my legs. "You poisoned one marriage for me and I want you to leave this one alone. You be polite to my wife. She didn't have to come here. She was frightened of coming. You asked us to come. Well, we're here."

She laughed—I had forgotten that quick noise of gaiety, produced on the intake of breath, with which she greeted the unexpected. "All I was saying," she said, "was that the boy's brains must come from the father."

"I wouldn't know. I've met the father only once."

She sighed.

"Don't mind me, Joey. I'm just an old crazy woman who's gone too long without talking to anybody except her dogs. I thought I could talk to my son but apparently I've presumed."

This tactic, of self-accusation, though familiar, was still formidable; my indignation dissolved in that inky mixture of bathos and clownishness and, to keep myself from conspiring with her, I left. "I must say good night."

"Sleep tight, Joey."

"Pleasant dreams, as Grandpa used to say."

"Pleasant dreams."

I left the living room, where the moonlight had begun to pick up as if in theft trinkets and silver edges, and groped my way up the steep cool country staircase. Richard was breathing smoothly. I dragged my fingertips across the side of his head. Back in New York I must get him a haircut. Entering our bedroom, I felt its darkness as the reverse side of an acute visibility; virtually blind, I felt myself viewed through the two sets of blue panes giving on the moonstruck meadow. In the far window, distorted by a wobble in the glass, there was suspended, like something shining in a recess of the sea, the red toplight of the television transmitting antenna recently erected, braced by wire stays, near the Turnpike. Under the faint pressure of remote light the room resolved into its components: windows, mantel, bureau, mirror, bed. The bedposts showed as silhouettes whose pineapple knobs crescentally bubbled into a third dimension, but the space of the bed was totally obscure: a rich hiatus, a velvet lake, between pale indications of deep windowsills. I touched a chair and undressed beside it. "Where are my pajamas?"

The mysterious space of the bed creaked and Peggy asked, "Do you want to bother with them?"

"Will we be warm enough?"

"Let's try it."

When I got into bed, she asked me, "What happened?"

"Nothing much."

"You're trembling like a puppy. Are you putting it on?"

I found and seized and pinned her wrists, as if she might try to roll away from what I had to say, and, my body half upon hers, our faces so close I felt her mouth as moist breath and saw by the glinting whites that her eyes were staring, said down into her, "I'm thirty-five and I've been through hell and I don't see why that old lady has to have such a hold over me. It's ridiculous. It's degrading."

"Did she say anything about me?"

"No."

"She did."

"Let's go to sleep."

"Is that what you want?"

"Aren't you too tired?"

She made no verbal answer. There is a merciful end to words.

———

MY WIFE IS WIDE, wide-hipped and long-waisted, and, surveyed from above, gives an impression of terrain, of a wealth whose ownership imposes upon my own body a sweet strain of extension; entered, she yields a variety of landscapes, seeming now a snowy rolling perspective of bursting cotton bolls seen through the black arabesques of a fancywork wrought-iron balcony; now a taut vista of mesas dreaming in the midst of sere and painterly ochre; now a gray French castle complexly fitted to a steep green hill whose terraces imitate turrets; now something like Antarctica; and then a receding valley-land of blacks and purples where an unrippled river flows unseen between shadowy banks of grapes that are never eaten. Over all, like a sky, withdrawn and cool, hangs—hovers, stands, *is*—is the sense of her consciousness, of her composure, of a non-committal witnessing that preserves me from claustrophobia through any descent however deep. I never felt this in Joan, this sky. I felt in danger of smothering in her. She seemed, like me, an adventurer helpless in dark realms upon which light, congested, could burst only with a convulsion. The tortuous trip could be undertaken only after much preparation, and then there was a mystic crawling by no means certain of issue. Whereas with Peggy I skim, I glide, I am free, and this freedom, once tasted, lightly, illicitly, became as indispensable as oxygen to me, the fuel of a pull more serious than that of gravity.

"Can we sleep?"

"The silence is so loud."

"There's an Indian blanket in the bureau. Shall I get it?"

"Do you need it?"

"Not if you don't leave me."

"Hey. I just thought of why I said you were like a puppy. You have a funny little doggy smell from feeding them. I like you as a country boy."

"Aren't you beautiful? I love your cunt."

"Love my cunt, love me."

"If you insist." I was drifting asleep.

My mother had wished me pleasant dreams. That night I redreamed for the tenth or so remembered time a small vision which had first broken upon my sleeping mind in the days when the possibility of divorce and remarriage was dawning upon my waking thoughts. I was home, on the farm. I stood at the front of the house looking up over the grape arbor, where the grapes were as green as the leaves, at the bedroom windows like a small boy, too shy to knock at the door, come to call on a playmate. Her face appeared in the window, misted by the screen. Peggy was wearing, the straps a little awry on her shoulders, a loose orange nightie I liked, and as she bent forward to call to me through the screen her smile was wonderful; she was so happy here, so full of delight in the strangeness of this place, so in love with the farm and so eager to redeem, with the sun of her presence, the years of dismal hours I had spent here. Her smile told me to come up; its high bright note assumed and summed up our history of fear and sorrow and considered ruthlessness; it knowingly conveyed, through itself from elsewhere, forgiveness—and it was so gay. Never had the farm been so gay.

I awoke and, as can be the case, the difference between dream and reality was a minor one of transposition. I was in the bedroom and Peggy's voice was below. Brightness came from outside; morning sunshine, muted by the mesh of the screen, lay at an angle on the broad sills. Unseen hands had placed the Indian blanket over me. The picture of myself as a boy smiled dimly on the wall, my limp collar melted, by once-fashionable darkroom trickery, into the utter white of the photographic stock. The voices downstairs circled unintelligibly around spots of laughter. I found in an empty closet a pair of my father's dungarees that were big on me. By turning the cuffs up and bunching the waist under a belt of my own I made them fit. In one pocket I found a tenpenny nail my father had bent to form some sort of a tool.

After years of what my father had called "primitive living," we had, under the necessity of my grandfather's final illness, created a bathroom upstairs out of the old sewing-room. The fixtures seemed smaller than life-size and the toilets flushed with a languor remote from the harsh gush of urban plumbing. On the room's one windowsill, which did for a cabinet, there remained, among my mother's gaudy array of pill vials and the rather embarrassing variety of hygienic items Peggy had unpacked, my father's razor. Made heavier than they are made now, it had a turquoise patina of verdigris. Its top unscrewed into sandwichlike components, the blade being the meat. I inserted a blade of my own and shaved with it; its angle scraped and burned and, just as my father had always done, I nicked the curve of my jawbone. The cut and blood and sting were satisfying, and I remembered the queer sheep's smile my father would wear coming downstairs with bits of shaving soap still attached to his ears, like tags. Shaving himself clumsily was one of the many small self-neglectful acts with which my father placated the spectre of poverty: I had not understood this before. I had never advanced so far into his skin as now. I always experience, on the first morning when I awake at home, a tonic, light-hearted uncertainty as to exactly who I am.

In the room where Richard had slept, the photograph of Joan, voguish and posed, was flattened by daylight into the same plane of remoteness as the one of myself as a child; ten years faded level with thirty under the bright present of this cloudless morning. Downstairs, on the tawny kitchen floorboards scuffed and scored by dog claws, there lay, like a papery golden mat spread before the front door that gazed with its single large pane through the grape arbor toward the meadow, a rhomboid of sun mottled with the slightly shivering shadows of grape leaves. This patch of sun had been here, just this shape, twenty years ago, morning after morning.

Peggy was making pancakes. Richard and my mother sat at the table, the boy eating cereal and my mother drinking coffee. Something in the deliberate way she was holding the cup eclipsed the others for me, though Peggy looked up and grinned and Richard was brightly talking. He was telling the plot of the science fiction story with which he had read himself to sleep. Peggy was wearing pigtails. Her long hair, which becomes red in the summer and chestnut in the winter, which can be a mane or a beehive, a schoolmarmish bun or a drooping Bardotesque bundle, had been knitted into two stout jutting pigtails secured by rubber bands. I wondered if my mother found this hairdo presumptuous or too assertive or condescending. The fragrance of pancakes hung in the air like an untaken gift, and Richard seemed to be talking to himself. ". . . and there was this one man left in all the world, crawling over these warm cinders, trying to get to the sea."

Peggy asked me, "*Where* did you get those baggy old pants?"

"You've cut yourself," my mother said. There was an evenness in her voice like the gray of the sky on a day before rain.

"I shaved with Daddy's razor."

"What a funny thing to do. Why?"

Had I somehow interfered, desecrated a shrine? "It looked too lonely," I said, "sitting there."

My mother turned her head and released me from the threat I had felt. Her voice relaxed, swerved. "I should throw it away but I like the color it's become."

I walked forward boldly. "Who's the pretty slave making pancakes?"

"Isn't she clever? She found a box of mix I had forgotten I had. And they smell so good."

"My father," Richard said, "can make terribly thin little ones with just flour and water over a camp fire."

"He sounds too clever," my mother said.

I said to Richard, "What's this story you were telling about warm cinders?"

Peggy called, above a fresh salvo of sizzling, "It sounds like a very morbid story to read just before going to sleep."

"There's been atomic war or something," Richard said, "it never exactly says, and there's this single man, the last man left on the planet Earth, crawling over the radioactive desert to get somewhere, and then you realize he's trying to reach the sea. He hears it murmuring."

"Did you hear," my mother asked me, "the dogs last night around three o'clock? There must have been a deer in the neighborhood. Or else the Schoelkopfs' beagle went into heat suddenly."

"Can that happen so suddenly?" Peggy asked.

I said, "No, I slept right through. I always do, Mother, you know that. I'm a growing boy."

"Everything wakes me now," she said. "Even your bed seemed noisy to me last night."

"Maybe we should buy a muffler for it."

Peggy said, "Richard, he's crawling toward the sea."

"I'm sorry, Richard," my mother said. "Tell us."

"He gets to the sea, and lies down in it, and prepares to die with this feeling of great relief, because his idea was if he could die in the sea the cells of his body would keep on living and form the basis for new life, so evolution could begin all over again."

"I agree with your mother," my mother said. "That story is too frightening to read at bedtime."

"Who wants pancakes?" Peggy asked. "They're getting cold."

"That's not the *end*," Richard insisted, and his mother's voice emerged in his anxious intonation. "The clincher, the really neat thing, comes in the last sentence, when he lies down in the water and looks up and—I forgot to say it was night—and looks up and sees the stars but in totally different patterns from what they are now! You see, all along you thought it was happening in the future when actually it happened aeons and aeons in the past."

"I don't understand about the stars," Peggy said, smartly setting out plates and then dividing the pancakes among us with her efficient naked hands.

"I don't either, Peggy," my mother said. "I thought the stars were fixed."

"Mom, don't be dumb," Richard said. "The stars are changing position all the time but so slowly we can't see it. Some day Arcturus will be the North Star."

"Don't be fresh."

"I wasn't fresh. What's fresh about a fact?"

"I remember reading that story," I said. "What it comes down to is all of us, including the dinosaurs and the bugs and the oak trees, are all descended from that one man. Richard, do you ever at night, just before dropping off, feel yourself terribly huge? Your fingers feel miles thick."

"I often do," he said. "It's uncanny. I've read somewhere a rational explanation, I forget where. Maybe in *Scientific American*."

"Well, that's how that man must have felt lying there in the water dying, don't you think?"

"I suppose," Richard said, uneasy that the fantasy of the

book, which had seemed solely his, had been appropriated by us others.

"I think it was nice of the man," my mother said, "to care so much about his descendants. Peggy, these are too good. I'm supposed to go easy on starch."

"Eat all you can. There's tons of batter."

"I'll *bust*!" my mother exclaimed, and I had to laugh, for clearly, in her own mind, she was being, ingeniously, murdered.

After breakfast she and I went out to start the tractor. It was by then ten o'clock. Time on the farm always had an elusive elasticity. As a boy, my back sweating and my eyes raw from searching green leaves for spots of red, I would come down through the orchard from the strawberry patch, four full quart boxes balanced on my right arm and two more held in my left hand, after hours of straddling the endless rows of dense secretive leaves, and discover, by the mantel clock (it was still there but had stopped, like the clock in a song my grandfather used to sing, raising his voice on *"Tick. Tock"* and lowering it on the premonitory "And the old man died"), that it was only nine-thirty, the day barely begun. And yet that same day (there were so many such days), after a moment spent glancing at a magazine to speed the digestion of the lunch my grandmother had hastily scratched together, I would look up from the sofa and see the mailman's dusty Chevrolet at our box, half in the shadow of the barn, for it had become, in one swift stroke, the middle of the afternoon.

Now the day and the fields it contained seemed about to break over our heads like a tidal wave, with the tractor still asleep. My mother tried to hurry and touched her hand to her chest as her breath came up short. By daylight the lawn was painfully ragged with plantain and crabgrass.

The tractor, an ancient gray Ford with a narrow bonnet that suggested the head of a mule, used to wait under the homely overhang that my mother had at last pulled down. There, on the straw-strewn dirt and footworn stones of the barnyard, it was out of the rain but exposed to the wind which, on wet days, would fling and float into this space tingling intimations of the downpour. When I was young this space of shelter had for me a precious wild intimacy. Adze-cuts were still visible on the beams and posts; the tractor, ticking as its motor cooled, reminded me of live animals once housed here. Once I had stood here and watched my mother outrace my father to the house under the rain.

Now the tractor was kept in one of the stables, where the sunless air tasted of dung dust. My mother groped in the manger for the oil can and lubricated the tractor's joints with a hollow popping sound like mechanical suckling. I pried up the door of its bonnet and fed it gas. The gasoline, leaping lavender from the spout, turned through some alchemy of shadow brownish-gold inside the tank, and the can, as its liquid contents unravelled, fought my grip like a singing reel. My mother no longer trusted her strength to perform this operation. But it was she who started the motor. She set one foot on the running board, grabbed the cracked rubber wheel, and startlingly swung her heavy body up into the iron saddle. I, in the style of my father, when confronted with the delicate puzzle of a fading battery and a guesswork choke and an erratic fuel pump, tended to flood the motor. But my mother had developed a prehensile tact with the machine, and soon the antique engine crackled into life and roared with a violence that hurled swallows into the blue rectangle of sky which had been placed, now that the overhang was down, right at the stable door.

Pleased, she yielded her seat to me. The metal felt warm. I rehearsed the pattern of pedals, moved the fuel lever to a middle notch, let up on the clutch, and lurched monstrously into the open. My mother screamed and I yanked the lever that lifted the cumbersome cutter off the stones; it wagged and clanked behind me as I swayed onto the lawn.

Peggy and Richard stood on the porch to see me go by, a

one-man parade, an aging actor with half-gray hair and a soft city body absurdly being carried away by a juvenile role. They seemed quite abandoned by my success; I waved, and would have stopped, but my control of the machine was not yet instinctive and I might have stalled. Effortlessly strong, pulling a tugging hemisphere of space behind me, I went up the slant of lawn, across the rough walk, into the road, past the mailbox, toward the upper field. The great wheels revolved so slowly that, looking down, I could see the individual teeth of the treads swinging upward like the blank heads of an advancing army. I had not grown up with tractors, so they seemed marvellous to me. As their rickety little engines are plunged by parabolic gear ratios into a deep well of power, their power crests in an absolute tenderness, in the sensation of enthronement atop an immense obligingness.

In the field, I engaged and lowered the cutter. The tractor, hugging at every jog the uneven earth, accepted whatever direction I suggested to it and herbivorously moved toward distant lakes of Queen Anne's lace. Hay tapped the edges of metal by my feet. Mashing and creaking settled into my ears and became shades of silence; the covered cutter dragged behind the tractor laid down a mowed wake like a width of cloth. Swallows, gathering in the fleeing insects, flicked around me, as gulls escort a ship. The field was vast, yet the very slowness of my progress—my mother had taught me to favor the third gear, though my father used to mow in fourth, bouncing and skidding dangerously—subdued it, guaranteed that, once I had reached the remote line of weed trees, sumac and ailanthus, that divided the big field from the far field, I would, as steadily, return. My mother's method, when she mowed, was to embrace the field, tracing its borders and then on a slow square spiral closing in until one small central patch was left, a triangle of standing grass or an hourglass that became two triangles before vanishing. Mine was to slice, in one ecstatic straight thrust, up the middle and then to narrow the two halves, whittling now at one and now the other, entertaining myself with flanking maneuvers acres wide and piece-meal mop-ups. I imitated war, she love. In the end, our mowed fields looked the same, except that my mother's would have more scraggly spots where she had lifted the cutter over a detected pheasant's nest or had spared an especially vivid patch of wildflowers.

Black-eyed susans, daisy fleabane, chicory, goldenrod, butter-and-eggs each flower of which was like a tiny dancer leaping, legs together—all these scudded past the tractor wheels. Stretched scatterings of flowers moved in a piece, like the heavens, constellated by my wheels' revolution, on my right; and lay as drying fodder on my left. Midges existed in stationary clouds that, though agitated by my interruption, did not follow me, but resumed their mid-air parliament. Crickets sprang crackling away from the slow-turning wheels; butterflies loped and bobbed above the flattened grass as the hands of a mute concubine might examine, flutteringly, the corpse of her giant lover. The sun grew higher. The metal hood acquired a nimbus of heat waves that visually warped each stalk. The tractor body was flecked with foam and I, rocked back and forth on the iron seat shaped like a woman's hips, alone in nature, as hidden under the glaring sky as at midnight, excited by destruction, weightless, discovered in myself a swelling which I idly permitted to stand, thinking of Peggy. My wife is a field.

A speck of Easter-pink, my mother, appeared on the road as I was turning on the far side of the field. I continued along the edge I was mowing, heading toward her. It was near noon.

The hair on the top of my head felt like hay, and I began to sneeze, suddenly, unstoppably; every cubic inch of atmosphere seemed transparently crammed with pollen and, my vision choked, I nearly chewed up two quail who exploded into the air beneath my wheels. I had not noticed at first that Peggy and Richard were with my mother, and the dogs, running in wide delighted circles. I pulled up among them and shut off the ignition. My mother said, "You poor child, has it been this bad all morning?"

"Has what been bad?"

"Your hay fever."

"It just started when I saw you."

"When you saw us?" She turned to Peggy and said, "He says it's psychosomatic."

Peggy had brought me lemonade, in one of those old-fashioned canning jars with a wire handle fixed to the glass. In taking it from her, I made our fingertips touch, but saw no change in her expression, which was cheerful and guarded. She wore white shorts and a yellow sleeveless blouse darkened where the hems rubbed her perspiring skin. When I lowered the lemonade jar from my mouth, she licked, in a flicker of empathy that seemed to betray nervousness, her own upper lip, which was mustached with moisture. She did not respond to my mother's remark, but instead seemed intent upon me, as if trying to remember where we had met.

I asked her, "What have you been doing all morning? Is it time for lunch?"

My mother said, "You've been up here only an hour. We did the breakfast dishes and now we're taking the dogs for that walk around the farm we talked about. Do you want to come along?"

"I have to mow."

"You've done a lot. What gear are you using, Joey?"

"Third."

"Are you watching for birds' nests?"

"I haven't seen any."

"I saw you scare two quail coming in. How many rocks have you hit?"

"I did tick one up toward the corner."

"That big one. Daddy always took a piece out of it; you'd think it would be level with the ground by now."

Richard said, "Tractors are slow, aren't they?"

In my mother's face I saw that she was going to attempt something fanciful. She told Richard, "That's because they're like dying people, they have their feet *in* the ground instead of on top." She was trying to sink into me the hook of her approaching death.

Richard's face went empty; I was annoyed with my mother for confusing him. "Would you like to drive it?" There was more to my asking this unfortunate question than an impulse of rebuke, of vengeance toward my mother. I think of myself as a weak man; one form my weakness takes is to want other people to know what they can and cannot have. I can tolerate only to a limited degree the pressure of the unspoken. Whereas my mother is infinitely at home in the realm of implication, where everything can be revised, or disowned.

Richard's voice became insouciant. "I would, as a matter of fact."

"Absolutely not."

If Peggy had been less quick to speak, my mother might not have argued. "Why," she said, "Sammy Schoelkopf was riding tractor when he was half Richard's age and not one-tenth as smart."

"Yes, and he cut off Mitzi's legs," I said.

"When I went camping with my father," Richard said, "he let me steer the power boat on the lake."

"Absolutely not," Peggy repeated.

"Mother knows best, Richard," my mother said to the

boy. To me she said, testing the pull of her hook, "Don't you want to to put on a hat and walk the bounds with us? I'm afraid you'll get sunstroke."

"Mother, I want to *mow*. I'll mow until lunch." I would mow and my mother would get to know Peggy: this was our bargain. I demanded of the three others that they mingle without involving me. I feared I might lose myself amid their confused apprehensions of one another and I hoped, as my mother's hurt gaze left me and Peggy's lips went prim, that irritation with me would tend to unite them. They moved away, walking warily on the stubble; Peggy wore sandals that left the sides of her feet exposed, and my mother, head bowed, was inspecting my work for errors, for ruined nests, butchered birds. Richard began to run in circles like the dogs, chasing the wisps of milkweed flax that alternated with cabbage butterflies in the air. I noted with pride that both women were tall, sizeable. It seemed a sign of some wealth that I could afford to snub them, and this prosperity enriched my triumph of floating between the steady wheels that reduced all unruly flowers to the contour of a cropped field.

After five or six circuits I saw them emerge from the woods, tinted specks, and bob toward the house along the horizon of the slope of land that descended to the foundations of the abandoned tobacco shed. Bouncing dogs, jogging child, plodding women: my tractor's long slow turning as I watched them gave me the illusion of pulling the string of them tight.

Toward noon the sky, as if fainting, began to entertain mirages of translucent bluish clouds. A beginning breeze caused the sweat to dry with cooling rapidity on one side of my body. The green hay turned greasy in tone as cloudlets, one by one, dipped it in shadow, and the sky behind the woods acquired the sullen solid pitch that wallpapers long hidden behind a sofa reveal to the movers. Two dwindled rectangular armies of uncut grass, separated by twenty tractor-widths, still stood against me when Richard came up the road and called me to lunch.

At the corner of the field across the road, the little upper field, there was a tall old pear tree shaped like a ragged fountain. It had many rotten and useless limbs and concentrated its fruit-bearing on the surviving boughs; the crowded pears, though not yet ripe, were dropping abundantly. I parked the tractor in the tree's shade, on grass saturated with wormy, spicy fruit.

Richard and I walked down the road together. My father's dungarees felt stiff around my stride, my tingling palms were gray from gripping the baked rubber wheel, my vision felt sandy—all comfortable sensations, proof, as my real work never gives me, of work done. I asked Richard, "How was the walk?"

"Interesting. We saw a woodchuck and some kind of rare thrush. Your mother knows the names of everything."

"Just like you know all the Yankees."

"Yeah, but that's in the newspapers."

"There is that difference. I think my mother has some nature books you could ask her about if you want to."

"O.K."

"I could never match the pictures up with the real things, exactly. The ideal versus the real."

"That's an ancient philosophical problem."

"Or else just lousy pictures."

"This morning I was reading in that anthology about a mutie, that's short for mutant. There's been an atomic war—"

"Again?"

"It's a different story. This time, lots of people survive, but the radiation mixes up the genetics and most of the babies are born freaks, that's why they're called mutants. Most are mistakes, but some are improvements, people with four hands, and so on. It sounds silly—"

"No."

"The story is about a boy with a gigantic I.Q. who when he's eighteen months old reads the dictionary through to learn the language."

"But then can he match the words to the real things?"

Richard took my joke seriously. "I haven't finished the story yet, it's eighty-seven pages long." We walked a few silent steps in the dust. He said, "My father has a high I.Q."

"How did your mother like the walk?"

"O.K., I guess. She told me not to throw rocks and your mother said it was all right as long as I didn't throw them at anything living."

"Did your mother and my mother fight?"

"Huh?"

"Do you think they're getting along?"

"When we came back to the house your mother told my mother she better wash her feet with yellow soap or she'd have poison ivy."

"That doesn't sound exactly like a fight."

"I didn't say it did."

We still had a minute together, crossing the lawn to the back porch. I told him, "This afternoon I'll try to find my old softball bat and we can hit some fungoes. I used to hit a tennis ball against the barn and then try to catch it before it hit the ground. If it bounced once, it was a single, and so on."

"You can make up lots of games to play by yourself if you have to."

"I had to. I almost never had a playmate here."

"What about Charlie?"

"Not counting my own children."

"Frankly, I'd rather help you mow," Richard said.

"We'll discuss it."

We reached the pump. How beautiful water is! Nothing, not the slaking of lust or the sighting of land, appeases a deeper creature in us than does the satisfaction of thirst. I drank from the tin measuring cup that my mother had care-lessly left on the bench one day and that under the consecra-tion of time had become a fixture here. Its calibrated sides became at my lips the walls of a cave where my breath rustled and cold well water swayed. Against my shut lids the blue sky pressed as red; I would gladly have drowned. My gratitude to the elements went indoors and embraced the women making lunch in the kitchen. Peggy's pigtails had come down; her hair hung loose. Her bare feet, freshly washed, left damp prints on the floor. My mother had become, in the kinship of house-work, a docile, stupider sister. She set the placemats around while Peggy arranged, with naked quick hands, slices of cheese and Lebanon balony on an oval blue platter. The platter was one of a set my mother had assembled, plate by plate, at Tues-day Ladies' Nights at the Olinger movie house before the war. My mother's house was strange in that things lasted for-ever here; a dish was never broken. I felt her wince as Peggy smartly slapped plates and glasses on our placemats.

My mother cleared her throat and said, "When I worked in the parachute factory, there was a redheaded girl worked next to me who could cut and tie three to my one. When the D-Day invasion came, we were told to join hands and pray, and hold-ing her hand was like holding a bird; you know the way a bird's heart beats and they feel so dry and feverish. No won-der she could stitch like that. It quite frightened me."

Peggy laughed. "Maybe *you* frightened *her*."

My mother swung her shoulders and lifted her eyebrows, the way my grandfather would do when parried. "To tell the truth, I believe I did. I don't think until she met me she had ever known people could fumble so. She once told me, now that I remember, that she thought I was a refugee. When she first saw me, she thought I was a foreigner, and had been sur-prised I spoke English so well."

Richard laughed, perhaps too readily, and to intercede I asked, "Whatever happened to her?"

My mother said, "I used to wonder. I'm afraid nothing good. She had a child and no husband and wasn't yet nineteen. With a pulse like that she was bound to get into trouble. Just like a hurt starling, it was that rapid." My mother's facial expression troubled me, and I realized that she had taken to making pop eyes at the end of a statement, the way old people in Pennsylvania do. In my grandfather this rhetorical condition had been exaggerated by the bulging lenses of post-cataractomy spectacles.

"Soup's on," Peggy said, pouring. Steam rolled up the length of her arm and mixed with her hair. She returned the pot to the stove with a click and we settled at the table. The soup was chicken-with-rice.

Seated in my father's position, I asked Peggy paternally, "Did you see the farm this morning?"

"It's lovely," she said, and, turning slightly to include my mother, "I like knowing its boundaries. I had the impression last night it was enormous, but seeing it in daylight it doesn't seem too big."

"Just big enough," my mother said, nodding eagerly, as if to certify Peggy's remark before it escaped. "Just the right size. I don't think God *meant* people to live on *less* than eighty acres."

"Statistically, most of them do," Richard said.

"I know," my mother told him. "It makes me sad to think of it. I don't know why I'm so fortunate. I certainly don't deserve it." She waited to be contradicted.

"By the year twenty-one hundred," Richard said, "each person will have about one square yard of land to stand on, including all the deserts and mountain tops."

"I *know*," my mother said, and I inwardly shied from her fervent intonation. "I *see* it coming. You can see it in Alton, the people are growing corners so they can fit in their little square yards better. People were meant to be *round*."

Richard said, "I recently read a story where the people were shaped like cones and the doorways were all triangular."

"Plato says," my mother told the boy, "that God made people absolutely round, with four arms and four legs and two heads, and they would roll everywhere with terrific speed. In fact, people were so happy and powerful that God grew jealous and split them in half, with a little difference, so that now everybody keeps looking for their other half. That's what love is."

"What was the difference?" Richard asked.

My mother said, "It's a very little difference."

"You mean the penis?"

The word had never been used in my childhood—there had been instead, strange to recall, the non-word "animule." I remember my mother saying, when my father and I were dressing in the morning and she still lay in bed, "My men have such big animules." I felt her feigned fright was partly sincere, which seemed absurd, since mine was smaller than my thumb, and I never looked at my father's. Richard had shocked my mother.

She said to him, "Yes."

"There are psychological differences, too," Peggy told him.

My mother, who liked to do her own amplifying, said, "I've never believed in those. I'm a very coarse customer. I believe only in what I can see or touch."

"And God," Richard said.

My mother's head dipped forward in surprise and, as if to make something useful of the gesture, she took another slice of balony. "God?"

"We discussed it before we came. He"—me—"said you believed in God."

"And you don't?"

Richard looked at us, at Peggy and me, for help, which came, instead, from my mother. She said, "I see and touch

God all the time." The froglike shininess of fascination returned to his eyes as he looked at her. She went on, "If I couldn't see and touch Him here on the farm, if I lived in New York City, I don't know if I'd believe or not. You see, that's why it's so important that the farm be kept. People will forget that there could be anything except stones and glass and subways."

"There are lots of farms in Nebraska," Richard said.

"I don't live in Nebraska."

"We saw lots of farms driving up the Turnpike."

"I don't care about those farms. I care about *my* farm."

The child, with a silent effort that thinned his lips, located the problem correctly, not in a national passing of farmland but in my mother, personally. He returned to his original question, with a difference. "What can you use it for?"

My mother pointed at me while looking at Richard. "He says a golf course is too expensive."

"Where my father took me there was lots of wild land being kept as a bird sanctuary. But there was a lake in it."

"We can call this," my mother said, "a *people* sanctuary."

As if to laugh, Richard showed his teeth with the neat frontal gap, but no sound emerged.

"A place," my mother went on, "where people can come, and be refugees like me, for an hour or two, and let their corners rub off, and try to be round again."

This cloying ingenuity, holding the boy spellbound with its undertone of desperation, became unbearably pathetic and irritating to me. "Mother," I said, "you do exaggerate the land shortage. If you'd ever fly in an airplane you'd see how much of it there is. Land is worthless until people make something out of it."

"Hush," she said. "Richard and I are planning a people sanctuary. I'll sell tickets up at the pear tree and he'll be the warden and mark the diseased people for destruction."

"What a funny sanctuary," Peggy said. "Like a concentration camp."

"Peggy," my mother said, her eyes suddenly saturated with tears and reflected light, "people must be told when they're no longer fit to live, they mustn't be left to guess at it, because it's something nobody can tell herself." And she left the table and the kitchen, slamming the screen door, her pink blouse clashing with the green outside.

———

ALL AFTERNOON the signs of a storm gathered. The translucent clouds developed opaque bellies and were hurried sideways by a rising wind. From my stately tractor I admired, what I had forgotten, how dramatic the clouds in this hill country could be. Diagonal shafts of sun and shadow and vapor streamed earthward from glowing citadels of cumulus spaced as if strategically across the illusory continent above; the spectacle was on the high grand scale of history, so that the elidings and eclipsings and combinings of cloud-types suggested political situations—high thin cirrus playing the aristocrat, a demagogic thunderhead moving at the head of an amorphous gray mob. My mother's display of temper, or grief, hung heavily on the afternoon. After the door had slammed, Peggy had asked, "Did I say anything?"

"I don't know, did you?"

"What did I say?"

"Nothing really. You were saying what you thought."

"Shouldn't I? It seemed to me she deliberately decided to take it personally."

"With my mother, everything is personal."

"If it hadn't been that, it would have been something else I said. She turns it on and off, she uses her temper as a weapon."

"When you're as sick as she is you'll use what weapons you can."

Richard asked, "Shall I go ask her why she's mad?"

"You can if you want," I said, startled and touched by his volunteering. At his age I had felt myself the family peace-maker; indeed this role had ceased only when my father died. "She likes talking to you about the farm."

"I like listening. I like it here." He glanced at Peggy and turned, and the screen door slammed a second time, behind him.

Peggy, beginning to clear the dishes, asked me, "What shall I do?"

"What do you mean?"

"I mean what shall I *do*, do this afternoon. Do to get through this horrible visit."

"Do what you want to do. Read a book. Take a sunbath." A break in a coalition of cloud had released a flood of sunshine on the bits of greenery I could see through the back door pane—some orchard grass, some lawn grown tufty around two stepping-stones, an overhanging walnut-tree limb, a sallow hydrangea bush months past bloom.

"I don't know," she said, brushing back her hair from her face, "it all seems too complicated."

I said, "Too complicated for *what*? Just try a little tact." I could not account for the anger in my voice.

Richard's face appeared at the screen door, calling in, "Mother, I'm going to hoe with Mrs. Robinson. She's going to teach me how to tell weeds. We'll be in the garden above the orchard."

"Don't get sunstroke," Peggy said.

My mother's face appeared in the screen door above Richard's. Behind the mesh her face was almost featureless, the head of a goddess recovered from the sea. "Don't mind me, Peggy," she called in. "You're quite right about the concentration camp. That's my Teutonic sense of order. Just stack the dishes, I'll do them later." Their footsteps scuffed off the porch.

As Peggy reached across me for a plate, I stroked her breast, pushed toward me by her stretching, and said, "Alone at last. Let's fuck."

"You smell like hay," she said. "You'd make me sneeze." I felt in her body a repellent tension and so left her to go mow among the clouds.

The idyll of mowing grew weary with the day, which moved slowly. When mid-afternoon seemed reached, I went down to the porch for a drink of water, and discovered, in the empty house, that the electric clock said only ten past two. The dishes were washed and put away. Behind the house, in the side yard, where the grass was always soft and easiest to mow, Peggy lay in her bikini on the Indian blanket, sleeping.

"Are you asleep?"

"No."

"Are you happy?"

"So-so."

"Where's my mother and your son?"

"Aren't they hoeing?"

"I didn't see them in the patch."

"They must be somewhere."

"Haven't you gone and talked to them all this time?"

"I just came out here a half-hour ago. I've been doing the dishes and cleaning. There are cobwebs in every corner. Does she ever sweep?"

"*Her* mother used to be very energetic so I guess she never got into the habit."

"Why are you always making excuses for her?"

"It's not an excuse. It's a rational explanation, as Richard would say."

My wife, who had been lying on her front, her hair thrown

upward off her back as if she were falling through space, rolled over, so her belly went incandescent in the sun, and she flung a downy forearm across her eyes. Her lips parted under the thrust of the sun on her skin. I said, "I love you."

Her thighs were enough spread to reveal stray circlets of amber pubic hair. Her fair body, its nakedness barely broken by the knotted bits of polka-dot mauve, twitched like the body of a fretful child who has been touched. I did not dare touch her. She spoke without taking her forearm from her eyes. "Well you don't make me feel it here. You're so—how shall I say?—*busy*. I feel you're emotionally fussing at us all the time and making everything worse."

"I didn't know things were bad."

"Of course they're bad, you expected them to be."

"Richard seems to be having a good time."

"She's playing up to him as a way of getting at me some-how. Anyway, I need cigarettes and I'm getting the curse."

"Do you have Tampax?"

"No, I need that too. I'm early and didn't bring any."

"Maybe my mother has some."

"I don't think she's that much of a marvel, sweetie."

I blushed, having forgotten that it was many years since my mother had filled the house with the secret rage of her men-struation. As a child in Olinger I was once rebuked for playing by the wastebasket with these white toy telescopes. Standing there foolish, in my father's baggy pants, I nevertheless expe-rienced a regal desire to give Peggy a baby and thus stanch her bleeding. I said, "I'll tell her we have to organize a shop-ping expedition."

"I thought we passed a little store about a mile before your lane."

"That was Hartz's. It's run by some Mennonites and they don't sell cigarettes. The nearest cigarettes are five miles toward Alton, at Potteiger's in Galilee."

"Galilee?"

"That's its name. You're in Bible country here."

So it seemed: I looked up from her body toward the meadow and saw the intervening trees (a young locust, a black walnut, a blue spruce that had once been no taller than I) and the grass of the lawn drenched in a glistening stillness, an absolute visual silence like a full-measure rest in the flow of circumstance, each waxen leaf and silvered blade receiving the hazed August sunlight so precisely my heart beat double, as if split. Then my vision was gently eroded by awareness of the insect and bird song that form a constant undercurrent to country silence.

The sun went in. Peggy kept her arm across her eyes. The mailman's car drove up the road, spinning a cloud of pink dust. I ran out to the mailbox and there was nothing in it, nothing except a junk circular for Boxholder and a windowed envelope to my mother from Dr. I. A. Graaf. My mother and Richard were coming down through the far end of the orchard; they had been in the upper end of the strip of woods between our land and the torn fields waiting for ranch houses. I cut through the lower orchard to hand her the mail and to discuss the need to shop.

"We just saw some fox droppings," Richard announced. "They're darker and thinner than the woodchuck's."

"The foxes are getting plentiful again," my mother said. "They go in cycles with the pheasants, and we're in a fox phase now. Five years ago the pheasants would come right to the back door." She squinted toward the side of the house, where Peggy lay. "I hope Sammy Schoelkopf doesn't have his binoculars out," she said.

I said, "I told her to take a sunbath. She did all the dishes and dusted the living room."

"Fine," my mother said, laughing lightly and rocking backwards from my sharp tone, "fine. I'm all for Nature, the more of it the better."

"We need cigarettes."

"I thought you stopped smoking."

"I have. Peggy needs them."

"You should tell her, tobacco makes the teeth brown."

"Mother doesn't inhale," Richard said. "My father laughs at the way she smokes."

"When does he see her to laugh at?" I asked.

"When he comes for me and brings me back."

"Peggy also needs," I told my mother, "a female thing."

"Oh?"

"So somebody ought to shop. How much do you still like to drive?"

"No more than I have to. Since June I'm afraid of a spell. I don't mind myself going out with a bang, but it seems unkind to be a menace to the other cars."

"O.K., I'll drive. Do we need any food?"

"Probably. Let me look in the icebox and talk with Peggy."

Her saying "icebox," though it was a refrigerator, took me again back to Olinger, a child's world where the simplest expeditions were exciting and Tampaxes were toys. I told her, "You organize an expedition. Everybody can come if they want. I'll go mow until you're ready."

My mother put her hand on my forehead, testing for a fever. "Now don't overdo. Remember you're a city boy now."

"Sometimes when he brought me back," Richard told me, innocently proud of having not been neglected, "he used to spend the night and have breakfast with us."

They went on down to the house. My mother stooped to retrieve a hoe from the long grass. Peggy got up from the blanket to greet them. Perhaps I imagined the whorish little hitch of her hips as she stood erect, and the arrogant flick of her hair back from her eyes. I had met her first husband just once, in New Haven, when we retrieved Richard from him on the drive back from our Truro honeymoon—two weeks containing ten days of rain. The decaying stairs on the sand cliffs of the outer beach had seemed Jacob's-ladders to me and the variety of smoothed pebbles miraculous; the drizzly mist made our bodies vague except to each other and I had been imprudently happy, so happy my heart seemed to trespass the limits set to joy. At night, when Peggy fell asleep beside me in the little rented cottage furnished with wicker armchairs and wartime-edition detective novels and ashtrays that were quahog shells, the roof muttered in the rain and my mind would wander in the encircling desolation where things necessarily end. Our little lease expired. Richard's father—McCabe, she always called him, never using his first name—was an assistant dean at Yale. Prepared to hate him, I confused myself by liking him. No taller than Peggy, ruddy and shy and balding, he had the tremulous yet smug air of the born academic. My mother had wanted me to become a poet or, failing that, a teacher; in the end I had disappointed both her expectations. Here in McCabe I confronted what I might have become. He had an unnatural physical youthfulness. Tennis and squash had conditioned his terse springy motions. The strange redness of his very neat lips suggested something vampirish to me, as if he were feeding off of his students. His smile was professionally ready. Like Richard he was engagingly gat-toothed and his eyes, of a deep clouded humorless brown, seemed prepared to receive a child's draught of unhappiness. The habit of interview carried from his job into his encounter with us in the form of an uncanny attentiveness betrayed, when Peggy's voice nervously reached too high, by a fiddling pronation of his wrists in his shirt cuffs. His manner with his ex-wife, while fond and sane, seemed above all wary.

This meeting left me with a need to understand better who had divorced whom. I had gathered that Peggy had decided, Peggy had insisted, Peggy had fought free; but from the humorless glint in Dean McCabe's round brown eyes I had received a disturbing contrary impression reinforced by the puzzling emphasis of his parting handshake. It seemed to be trying to squeeze too much into this moment of contact—

pity, forgiveness, competitive self-assertion, a relief that I had somehow proved harmless, gratitude, hatred, what? I could never get out of her what had been wrong with him. *We just weren't temperamentally well-suited. I felt it first and McCabe was nice enough to agree.* But what was your complaint exactly? Was he cruel? Did he philander? *No, not really.* Not really? *Not until I drove him to it.* You drove him to it? *Not consciously at first.* She tucked back her hair. But was he impotent? *Of course not. Don't be silly, Joey.* Her refutation seemed excessive, an unfeeling reflex mechanically ingrained by habits of self-defense. I hadn't really been asking her to tell me that they never made love. Or had I? But what did he fail to do for you then? *I don't know. I can't express it. He didn't make me feel enough like a woman.* But I do? *Of course.* But how? *You act as though I'm yours. It's wonderful. It's not something a man can do deliberately. You just do it.* And he didn't? *He was conceited and timid. I was a burden to him. He liked books and other men.* Is that why he hasn't remarried? All she had to say was Yes, but she said, *That, and I suppose*—blithely—*he thinks he's still in love with me.*

The clouds surrounding her divorce became the clouds I moved beneath, mowing. The sky that had seemed a nation of citadels and an arena of political maneuver verged on divulging the anatomy of a dead marriage: a luminous forearm seemed laid in sleep across a darker anatomy; the gathering nimbus suggested platoons of somber lawyers; the edge of a glowing, boiling protest told too sharply against a dwindling patch of blue. I struggled to dispel the thought, atmospherically encouraged by my mother, that I had been a fool, that McCabe's attitude toward me had been pitying and amused. If Peggy had slept with him after their separation, after their divorce, it could only mean she had wanted him back, and in the end he had not come.

A horn honked.

My mother was driving up the road in my father's old

Chevrolet. I parked the tractor in the open and brushed the chaff from my shirt. Richard was in the front seat beside her. I asked, "Where's Peggy?"

"She decided not to come. She would have had to change clothes."

"Did you ask her nicely?"

"Very nicely, didn't I, Richard?" My mother moved over, so I could drive.

"She said," Richard said, "she'd just as soon not come if we didn't need her."

I was suspicious of them both. "How unfriendly. Will she be all right alone?"

"Oh my goodness," my mother said, "we'll be gone fifteen minutes. She'll have the dogs to protect her. I've been alone here every day for seven years and every night for a year and I've never been approached."

"Well—"

"But I don't have as much to tempt evildoers, you're going to say?" She was agitated and reckless. Before I could soothe her, she went on, "Why don't you stay then and let me and Richard go, though what they'll think I want with Tampax I can't imagine. But never mind, they think I'm crazy in Galilee anyway. I must say Peggy impresses me as more able to take care of herself than any of us."

I got in beside her and let out the clutch and, still attuned to the tractor, made the old Chevy buck clumsily. My father's headlong and heedless style of driving seemed still to live in its metal. We went up the dirt road to the paved township road and from there back onto the state highway that yesterday had brought us south from the Turnpike. It continued toward Alton. After a mile the macadam road we had always travelled was swallowed by a new four-lane highway with a median strip of gray-blue spalls. White posts bore keystone-shaped reflectors. Between smoothly blasted banks of red rock the superhighway plunged through the hill the old road had skirted and carried us toward Alton in a way totally unfamiliar to me; it was magical. We seemed to skim free of any contact with the earth.

"Where are we?" I asked.

My mother said, "This is the back of Benjy's farm." Benjy was a Hofstetter, a cousin of hers, and of mine. "The state gave him a handsome sum," she added proudly. The land my father and I had travelled so often, back and forth to school, had been abolished, and for the shaggy curves and intimate quick vistas and postered barn walls sequentially fixed on the scroll of our pilgrimage had been substituted certain vague sweeping images of faded unfarmed grass and slashed clay. My mother, far from feeling lost as I did, seemed exhilarated, and pointed out that with the new arrangement of roads it took as long to get to the halfway town of Galilee as to the shopping center on the outskirts of Alton itself.

At my mother's insistence we went to the shopping center. The garish abundance, the ubiquitous music, the surrealist centrality of automobiles made me feel, emerging from my father's dusty car, like a visitor from the dead. I remembered these acres as a city dump adorned with pungent low fires and rust-colored weeds. In the supermarket nothing smelled, because even the turnips were bagged in cellophane, and the air had the faintly sour coolness of plastic. The greed my mother and Richard exercised in the aisles with my money exasperated me. I burned to return to Peggy, fearing that by some cruel rerouting of time she would have aged or vanished and I would be left with nothing but this present, this grim echo of my mother and this lonely child impersonating me—how eager to please we are, setting out in life!—amid this acreage of brightly shoddy goods.

Richard and my mother dawdled, and the checkout lines were long, and when the bags were in the car I said that Peggy this evening might like a gin-and-tonic. The liquor store, state-owned, was on the other side of the parking lot. The tar in softening had tugged the painted lines this way and that. Richard and my mother went into a Sun Ray drugstore to buy him sunglasses. Our absence lengthened maddeningly. By the time we got home we would have been gone over an hour. Speeding back on the broad white road whose magic already seemed obsolete, I remembered my wife in poses of suffering. I recalled that long period, which I preferred to forget, when for two years my indecision had subjected her to a series of disappointments and humiliations. I saw her again on the pale Sunday morning in early March when, after the exhausting Saturday night of my confession to Joan, I met Peggy in the Park. Richard wobbled up and down the path on the Christmas bicycle that in thrift she had bought too big. I told her I had promised Joan to wait half a year before any decision, six months in which, if the bargain was to have any meaning, we must not meet. Peggy had nodded, nodded, kept nodding in agreement as if it could not be otherwise and she were commending my judgment, my mercy toward Joan, my self-denial, so that I was stunned when she hurled her face against my shoulder and shouted into the cloth of my overcoat *Go, just go, Joey* and her storm of tears on the side of my neck had the heat of an assault and I realized that she had not been applauding my victory over my love for her but was herself that love, knew herself now in my love for her and saw herself abolished, saw us not meeting forever in a dwindling eternal width, which I then realized that I had not (the gray path, the few churchgoers black against the slush, the trees beginning to blur with buds, the Caribbean nursemaids in transparent galoshes) envisioned. And I remembered her naked, propping herself up in bed so her shoulders and slender neck were silhouetted against the loose hair translucent to the city glow from the window whose upper panes were blue, and her voice, suddenly thin, blurting, *Will you forget me?* And was it the following morning when I awoke, supposedly in Atlanta, and found it snowing in New York? At the height of her windows across the street each seed-ball clinging to the leafless sycamores wore a crescent of white. While dressing (in synchronization with my faithful double in Atlanta, who would be hurrying to catch a 9:40 plane), I put on the phonograph a record I had given her last night but that the emergency of love had not permitted us to play. It was Bach sung by a scat chorus: *Vo de oh oo oo, la la lalala.* As the bell-like voices poured hastening through the baroque score the wet snow hurried slantwise by the wind seemed to keep the same delicate pell-mell tempo, and Peggy made contraceptive ablutions in the bathroom, and I was transfixed, in trousers and a clean white shirt given a curious airy dampness by its supposed presence in a southern city; standing barefoot in the center of the soft Bolivian rug where we had lain, enraptured by the city beyond the windowsill where Peggy had scattered seed for sparrows, I felt my heart pinned at the point where the snow and Bach and her bathing intersected. I have never been so conscious of happiness, and so aware of the weakness of that condition, which partakes of delirium. When I left, in my business suit (my monogamous double was winging north), she abruptly begged, *Don't come again. I'm getting worse at saying goodbye. I'm sorry, I'm no good at this, I wanted to be a nice simple mistress for you but I'm not big enough. I'm too possessive. Go, go back and be nice to Joan. I've messed us all up by falling in love.* And when I first—prematurely—offered to leave Joan for her, she cried, *Oh no! Your children! I could never make it up to you!* Images recurred to me refracted, as if I had viewed her through thick glass. Meeting Joan at parties, her face had been brittle with fright and then defiance, and parting from me it had pinkly crumbled into weeping, and reuniting with me it had been pale with fatigue, and repeatedly she had taken me into her bed and her body as she might have taken an unavoidable sword; and I wondered, remembering, why I had made her suffer so much or, rather, by what right I had improvised our expiation. I pictured her helpless now, alone and raped, when her quota of grief had been fulfilled; I knew that the God who creates ironically would not scruple to impose this. My mother screamed. In a dream of rescue I had been driving too fast. My mother was skittish in cars; it was grotesque, how much she loved her life.

The broad white road, with one of those sweeping cloverleafs that seem histrionic, surrendered up the old black highway, and I turned onto the gray whirring surface of the township road, and then down our dirt road, and saw Peggy, and laughed, for she was on the garden ridge hoeing in her bikini.

The determination of her stance, the inexpert vigor of her blows at the ground, accented the width of her hips, which tapered to ankles that seemed to vanish in the earth. We stopped the car beneath the pear tree whose surviving limbs disproportionately put forth the full tree's burden of fruit. We got out of the car. The top of my head felt taut and ached. "What's so funny?" Peggy asked.

"You look lovely, Peggy," my mother said. "Don't let these men kid you. They want women to do their work for them and when you do it they laugh at you."

Richard had laughed loudest. "Mother, I don't think your costume is quite appropriate," he said.

My mother said, "Just be careful not to hoe up the beans, they have shallow roots."

"I tried to make my section look like yours," Peggy said, and with a dirty hand brushed back hair from her face. The sight of her bare feet, the toenails painted, flat on the earth and caked to the ankles like the feet of a child or a gypsy moved me; desire must have emanated from me as an odor or a wave of heat, for she cringed, embarrassed, and I realized I had exposed her, intensified the vulnerability of her costume.

"The top of my head hurts," I said, to distract my mother. "Are there any old hats of Daddy's I could wear?"

"You're getting sunstroke," she told me. "Don't mow any more."

"It has to be done."

"It should, but enough is enough. Don't punish me with it. You'll knock yourself out and then your wife will blame me."

"Mother, the sun has gone in. It's four o'clock."

"Peggy, do you think he should keep at it? His father would be stubborn about a job like this and then vomit all night. As if that was a treat for everybody."

"It can't be put off," I said. "Tomorrow's Sunday."

"What's happening Sunday?" Peggy asked, slapping at the gnats that scented blood between her thighs.

"My mother won't let anybody work on Sundays," I said.

"That's right," she said, "—poke fun of an old woman's superstitions."

Peggy asked her, "Do you really mind people working on Sunday?"

Now it was my mother I felt I had exposed. She said, "Around here it's considered a rather 'shidepoke' thing to do. But I suppose an old fool's weedy fields are like an ass in the ditch."

"Like a what?" Richard asked.

"It's in the Bible," Peggy told him.

My mother said to me, "It's up to you, Joey. I think you've mowed enough. Sammy can come over, or you can come back next weekend if you're determined to finish."

"But how *silly*," Peggy said, alarmed by the possibility of our returning so soon.

My mother turned on her. "Silly or not, when my boy looks like that it's time for him to quit."

I asked, "How do I look?"

"Pale and flushed."

"I can't look both. It's going to rain and I want to finish the big field at least. Let me have some pride of accomplishment. All I need is a hat of Daddy's."

"He never wore a hat. I'm surprised you've forgotten."

"I can mow," Richard said.

"There's an idea," my mother said. "Let the boy take a few turns. Show him how and you can watch from under the pear tree."

"Absolutely not," Peggy said.

"Oh come on, *Mom*. Let me. I'll be careful."

"Mother," I said, "now don't tease. You've got him all excited."

"I'm *not* teasing. If I could learn to run it when I was fifty Richard can learn now. If he can ride a bicycle in New York traffic he can do this."

I said, "A bicycle stops when you stop. A tractor demands a whole new set of reflexes."

"Oh please please *please*." Richard began to jiggle like a boiling pot and in his face as he looked up toward Peggy there flashed a timid eagerness that reminded me of his father.

"It's cruel of you," Peggy said to my mother, "even to suggest it. It's out of the question."

My mother's mouth flinched, making the quick noise of gaiety that she raised against the unexpected. "All the country boys by his age are old hands."

"He's not a country boy," I told her, interposing.

My mother turned to me gratefully and attempted to twist the matter upwards, into sheer fancy, and away. "How can Richard manage my people sanctuary if he can't drive a tractor?"

Peggy cut in. "He's not going to manage anything for you. He's not going to be another Joey." It was a reflex, ruthless and needless.

My mother, slashed, her subtlety crushed, said weakly, "Dear Peggy, one Joey is enough for me."

I said, "It's even enough for me."

Neither of the women laughed, and neither of them looked at me.

Richard had been listening without understanding that his fate was quite settled. He tugged at the lower half of Peggy's suit. "Just a lesson, Mother; just Lesson One, *Leçon Première*?" He was harking back to an educational television program they used to watch together in the days before me.

She squatted to him, her flesh spreading, the cavity between her breasts moist, and, encircling his waist with her long arms, said, "You may sit in the seat and work the levers, if the motor's turned off. But first I want you to go down to the house with your grandmother and help her take the groceries in."

"That's a good idea," my mother said. With held breath I felt the congestion in my chest loosen as the human clot around me broke. Richard got into the car and my mother drove it down to the house. I called after them for a hat. Peggy resumed hoeing. I touched the handle to still it. She said, "I'm sorry. She got me mad."

"Can't be helped. You pulled it out beautifully in the end."

"I'm still mad."

"Be mad at me."

"I am, partly."

"Why?"

"You don't stand up to anything. You let us slug it out and then try to make peace."

"I was on your side."

"I didn't feel it."

"It wasn't my mother's idea for him to ride the tractor, it was his."

"She encouraged it. It's an insane idea."

I thought "insane" excessive. "As she says, the boys around here do it."

"Insane."

"Tell me something. Did McCabe sleep with you after the divorce?"

Peggy stared and her dusty hand, in brushing back her hair, diagonally smirched her forehead. "Why do you ask?"

"Richard said, very happily, that his father spent the night a couple times."

When Peggy does not smile, the left side of her mouth tugs down with an automatic wryness. "He was safe. I knew him, and I thought it might do us both good."

"I'm sure it did."

She dismissed whatever was in my eyes with a shrug. "That piece of paper doesn't end everything."

"I know that. I know that very well. You seem to forget what a good position I'm in to know that."

"Well then don't look at me that way."

"I'm not trying to look at you any way. I see you as very beautiful, as having more beauty really than you need, and any waste makes me sad."

"All right then. I didn't want to go to waste."

"But at the same time you were seeing other men."

"Not then. This was soon after the divorce. It was years ago, Joey."

"Then why does Richard remember it so clearly?"

She looked down the line of the hoe-handle toward its idle teeth, and the fact that she was lying seemed declared by the comet-shaped smirch on her brow.

"It's funny," I said, "that I don't mind the others but do mind poor old McCabe, whom I kind of liked."

"The others aren't real to you," she said and, sensing that this explanation was tactless, added, "Or to me either now," and offered to kiss me. I accepted the offer; her lips felt like a pat of tepid dust. She put her arms, the same long pale-haired arms that had encircled Richard, on my shoulders, and told me, "Listen. This was all before you existed for me, it's like worrying about what happened before you were born. Don't you feel that I love you?"

I tried to be precise. "I feel you as a loving woman and I happen to be next to you in bed."

"No," she said, "that makes me a whore and it's really you, only you that lets me be a loving woman, because you know how to accept love, it's something your mother taught you. It's wonderful."

"It's a weakling's talent," I seemed obliged to say.

Richard was walking up the road with a hat. It was a hat belonging not to my father but to my mother, a wide coolie hat of plaited straw secured beneath the chin by a ribbon that was reinforced with butcher's cord. They laughed, Richard and Peggy, when I put it on. My fool's costume was complete. Richard and I went across the road to the stubbly field and I let him climb into the tractor saddle and showed him, ignition off, how the pedals and levers worked. He looked like a king solemnly enthroned against the nimbose sky and appeared satisfied. The lesson over, he went to the garden patch and joined his mother. He punched her stomach and I watched them pretend to box. Above them, on the single strand of wire strung to bring our house electricity, grackles and starlings neatly punctuated an invisible sentence. I mounted the tractor and resumed mowing. The chicory and goldenrod had curled their petals, had shrivelled under the threat of rain. A last piece of afternoon sun broke through the clouds and projected on the ground my grotesque shadow, my head a large globe. Within the hat there was a perpetual shade and the rustle of shelter. I moved the tractor into fourth gear and raced the weather. Once, the left wheel dropped into a ground-hog hole and the lurch nearly tossed me off. As I attacked my rectangles, my phalanxes of standing grass, a scouting buzzard below the clouds motionlessly rode the wind. Now a drop struck my forearm, and another tapped my hat. One standing section had been reduced to a long triangle and the other to a wavering hourglass-shape. I steered for the apex of the triangle, and back again along the hypotenuse, and back again. A heavy drop struck the gray hood and steamed. Another. Richard ran down the red road, but Peggy stayed on the garden ridge hoeing. The rain, having announced itself, hesitated, held off; I finished the triangle and went to the hourglass. A ragged, rapidly drifting wisp of smoky nimbus travelled at the base of advancing rolls of inverted gray. And now the rain, having taken one last breath, sighed and subsided into the earth, gently at first, like the blasts of a lady's atomizer, then with such steady relaxed force, pattering on my hat, soaking my thighs, that the closed flowers bobbed beneath the drumming and the grass, whipped, gleamed. I pushed the slipping tractor up one sloping side of the remaining phalanx, across the flat end, and down the other, until the waist of the hourglass vanished, and I was left with two triangles a few swaths wide. Turning the last time, I was astonished to see, at the far rim of the field, along the road, someone, Peggy, standing there in the storm watching me finish. She was holding her hoe and as I drew close I saw her red hair flattened against her skull and streaming straight around her face, which to endure the hail of sensation on her skin had assumed, lids stretched, cheeks puckered as if to smile, the imperviousness of the dead. She did not smile when, rattling onto the road at a rutted place below her, I called out, accusing her of insanity. She acknowledged me only by following the tractor, eyes downcast, like a nearly naked slave in processional chains, her shining feet picking their way carefully through the livid mud and the stones the rain was polishing to a sudden sharpness. I was so stirred by her faithful waiting, by the thought of her body beaten through and through by rain for my sake, that I expected, once the shelter of the overhang was reached, to leap from the tractor and embrace her, to press her into the chaff and dried dung, which would adhere blackly to her wet white skin. But the overhang was gone and while I was fitting the tractor back into its narrow stable Peggy continued across the lawn into the house, walked slowly across the stretch of grass where I had once seen my mother outrace my father from the barn. The afternoon had ended.

———

INSIDE THE HOUSE it smelled of Peggy's wet hair. My mother had laid and lit a fire of cherry logs in the fireplace and here my wife, out of her bikini and in a slip whose bosom and hem were lace, sat crosslegged, a blue towel across her shoulders, drying her hair. The fire seemed to saturate dangerously the veil of her hair; her head was thrown forward and her own fingers blindly massaged her scalp. The logs crackled, settling. Richard was reading a book; one leg was slung over the arm of the wing chair and swung like a pendulum. The rain breathed on the sides of the house, swept with an imperious gesture across the panes facing the barn, and lived sparkling amid the green and shuffling surfaces of the grape arbor outside the southern, meadow-facing windows. My mother in the kitchen was setting out plates. "Would they mind eating early?" she asked me softly as I went toward the stairwell.

"Ask *them*," I said. I felt that my mother in the garden had put Peggy in the wrong, had succeeded in illuminating her weaker side, and this triumph had shortened my patience with her. I would not have her feigning a conspiracy against these two strangers. Her games had cloyed.

Yet in the stairwell, hearing my mother's voice ask a question and Peggy's cheerfully answer, both with words I could not quite make out, I felt excluded and chilled. Upstairs I took off my wet clothes and walked naked through a glade of ghosts. The spot on the floor where my grandmother, trying to rise from her bed, had fallen and died shrouded its history in an inscrutable appearance of worn wood. The window still gave on the lawn, the barn, and the road as if my grandfather's eyes still watched for the mailman—the "snailman," he called him. A pine chest still hoarded his defunct stocks and his diaries, slim red booklets in which, year after year, he inscribed laconic notations of the weather and almost nothing else. On the day of my mother's birth, a day that almost killed his wife, he had only written, *Baby born.* As I draped them on the bathroom door to dry, my father's dungarees dripped icy water on my contracted loins. Joan still stared upward, a star of moisture frozen on her lower lip, the germ of a baby held forever in her belly. I did not use a towel; I love evaporation, not only the sensation but the idea of it, of moisture leaping freely into immateriality, of a topography in the elements whereby water slides downhill into air. Moving in air, I feel even dust, which makes me sneeze, as the sofa's angel, and pollen as immanent flowers. Dry, smooth, huge, immersed in the wide unfocused eyes of my childish self gazing from the wall, I put on underclothes, creased slacks slithery to the touch, socks Peggy had neatly balled in pairs, loafers, and a clean white shirt that seemed the wrappings of the rectangle of gray cardboard stiffening it.

Downstairs, my mother greeted my costume with, "There's my city slicker!"

At the supermarket she had bought a cellophane bag of peas she was now shelling. Each podful bounced musically in the colander. I sat down on the other side of the table and helped her shell. It was a peace gesture. Her shoulders were hunched over her task and she seemed for a time not to notice me. I finished the first heap I had taken and stood to reach into the bag for another. "Tell me," she said then, "how are they doing?"

"How is who doing?"

"Why, your children. Have you forgotten them so quickly? Ann and Charlie and Martha."

The little spheres, waxy green, pressed by their own fat fullness toward the shape of cubes in the pod, let go serially under my thumb and tumbled as a crowd into my palm. I made the colander chime and tried to answer. "All right," I said. "They always liked it in Canada and seemed pleased to be going there."

"Even without you."

"Well, I couldn't very well go *with* them. I was about to get married."

"Don't raise your voice like that. I have many afflictions, but I have not gone deaf."

"Good."

"I find myself," she went on, "remembering Charlie more clearly than the girls. He was such a vivid little man."

"Was?"

"Was for me. I don't expect ever to see him again."

"Sure you will."

"I thought he was going to be a farmer. He had just the right build, you know, those little wiry limbs and a barrel chest."

"He's surprisingly strong for being undersized."

"Oh, I *know*. To pick him up—almost the first time you brought him here, he was sitting daydreaming in Grampy's chair and I thought, 'Why, here's a cuddly little bundle,' and when I picked him up, he was a solid knot of muscles, hard as nails, and *not pleased*!"

I laughed. "Was this before or after you hit him with the yardstick?"

"He hit me, you mean. I think before, it may have been the same visit; but I doubt it. He gave me a very cold eye, I remember that. 'What do you mean, you big old lady, intruding on my repose?'"

"Funny the way he would daydream. One of Joan's aunts thought he was feeble-minded because he could sit still for so long."

"Why, he sat still because he had something worth thinking about. I never saw a little fella who was so deep." The word "fella" seemed to issue straight from my grandfather's mouth.

"Not even me?"

My mother considered. "No, you weren't meditative. You were *sens*itive. The first clear day in August you'd start sneezing and wouldn't stop until frost. Your eyes would run till they were pasted shut, it used to break my heart. Charlie had more of Joan's temperament—that frightening inwardness, that Puritan strength."

"She *was* strong. Always passively, though; she never initiated action."

My mother, sensing the presence of a complaint, curtly moved her hand, refusing to follow where I would have led. I was guilty of a hunger to become the center of this discourse. "Now Charlie," she said, "I could just imagine him, with that wonderful capacity for repose, waiting for the crops to ripen, and then rushing out with his hard little muscles and round chest to gather them in. He had what my mother called *bustle*. If you don't have it, like my dad didn't, you should get off a farm. Which is what he did, sensibly enough. I don't know why I could never forgive him for it."

"I'm scared for Charlie," I said. "He seemed to take it harder than the girls."

"They took it just as hard," my mother said, "but were better at concealing it from you. That's an idea you have, that women like to suffer. I don't know where you got it, not from me; they don't. But they get less sympathy than men because they have babies, and whenever a woman screams there's the thought, even in her own mind, that she's going to have a baby, so it's all right. Why a baby should make it all right I have no idea."

"Of the three," I said, "Ann in a way seemed most like me." Her face, Ann's face, its unpretty width and beautiful candor, her long straight legs and the way her mouth flared open in joy when she ran, recurred to me across what seemed a long anesthetic blankness, though I had never forgotten her name or her birthday or her existence. Charlie suddenly looked up at me. Was he eating an ice-cream cone? There was something silvery in the fineness of his straight brown boy's hair. Ann called him the Muskrat. His gray eyes were watchful, crinkled wisely at the corners almost like a man's, and his curved lips seemed ready to yield to a joke, though from his expression I was scolding him, or had puzzled him, by affirming something incredible; he was always ready, my son, to believe the best, to treat all grief—cut knees, his sister's teasing, my absences—as momentary nicks in a smooth extent of order. He was a tidy boy; much more than Ann did he fold and consider his clothes. And Martha, my baby: I not so much saw her as felt her loose weight when I would lift her, steeped in sleep, from her new blue bed, her tangled nightie, its cotton smooth as silk from contact with her flesh, swirling around her waist and exposing her genitals, paler than the moon with their dim cleft. I would lift her and carry her, her flushed head lolling, to the toilet and set her above the oval water and wait, sitting myself on the edge of the tub and letting her rest her head on my knee, for the hiss and modest splash. "Poor Martha," I said.

"Why, she's the toughest of the lot."

"She'll wet her bed."

"Of course she won't. She's a wonderful child. They're all wonderful children—aren't they, Peggy?" My wife had come into the kitchen and was standing beside and above me. From beneath she looked formidably tall, her nose somewhat hooked, her hanging hair expanded by being damp.

"Yes, they're nice," she said to my mother, "and I'm very sad about them too."

"Nobody's asked you to be sad. It makes us happy to talk about them."

"Joey went through hell over those children." My phrase, "through hell," sounded flat, as if she realized it was an echo. Peggy went on, "I'm sorry, I just don't see a need to remind him of them. He needs a rest."

My mother said, "A rest from remembering his own children?"

"What I really mean is please don't talk about the children as a way of getting at me. It's too hard on Joey."

"What a fancy idea! I talk about them, Peggy, when I do, because I'm a garrulous old misfit and because talk is the only way I can touch them now. I enjoyed being a grandmother, it was a curious comfort, an accomplishment I had never considered possible for me, I don't know why; and talking is the only way I can touch them now. Their father can visit them whenever he wants, but I don't expect ever to see them on Grammy's farm again. Or elsewhere."

"Oh sure you will," I said quickly, to stifle her terrifying threat of tears. "I'll bring them over this fall, when we're all back in the city again."

"Your wife won't wish you to," my mother said. Stemming her tears seemed to have dried her diction to a quaint stiffness. " 'Cleave to thy wife,' the Good Book admonishes."

"I intend to cleave to my wife," I said, "but I certainly expect you to see my children again."

"I have no such expectation; and for that matter, Joey, I don't expect ever to see you here again either." She turned to Peggy and said, "Thanks for coming this once, Peggy. And I liked your hoeing. You do careful work."

"Maybe I misunderstood," Peggy said. Her hardworking hands hung blood-heavy beside her thighs, touching lace. "But I know how Joey wants to hurt himself over those children, and I suppose I overreact when I hear their names."

My mother looked at me, my wife, and me again. Then she

: 77 :

put her palms flat on the table and pushed herself, so slowly she seemed to be growing, up off the chair, sighing. In such a moment, while changing physical position, she will often drop one of those casual remarks that let into a congested situation an unexpected amount of air. "Well," she said, "my parents stayed together without being happy and to tell the truth I'm not very grateful to them."

Standing, she turned her back and began to cook. Peggy offered to help, but my mother said she was ashamed of letting her guest do all the work. My mother's shape and face looked strange to me, lumpy and colorless, and I wondered if she were suffering pain. Pain in my parents had always been a difficult concept for me, like the galaxies beyond our galaxy. The rain whipped, caressed, embraced the house, made the wooden parts of it resound, set the shell of it afloat on seas of shimmering grass. I stood at the window looking toward the near woods. Thunder muttered from beyond where the owl had hooted. In my mother's ragged flower garden the phlox was being battered, letting white coins fall, and in the weedy caves at the feet of the passé hollyhocks hung small orange papery constructs, lantern-shaped, that I had not seen in any garden since leaving Pennsylvania. I asked my mother what they were and she said, "I don't know. We used to call them Japanese lanterns and then during the war the name was changed to Chinese lanterns. Now I suppose it's Japanese lanterns again." This window, giving on the most lonely side of the house, where the grass was softest and where Peggy had sunbathed, bore on its sill a toy metropolis of cereal and dogfood and birdseed boxes, whose city gates were formed by an unused salt-and-pepper set of aqua ceramic I had sent from Cambridge fifteen years ago. It was a window enchanted by the rarity with which I looked from it. Its panes were strewn with drops that as if by amoebic decision would abruptly merge and break and jerkily run downward, and the window screen, like a sampler half-stitched, or a crossword puzzle invisibly solved, was inlaid erratically with minute, translucent tesserae of rain. A physical sense of ulterior mercy overswept me and led me to turn; I avoided my mother's glance, lest with a boyish openness I overcommit myself to her again. Leaving the quieting cluck of her cooking on my left, I went into the living room, in search of the other children.

Peggy was sitting cross-legged before the fire again. She looked at me with eyes watery from the heat. Richard closed his book and his leg stopped swinging. "Well, that's a very surprising ending," he said.

I asked, "Is this still the story about the boy with the gigantic I.Q.?"

"Yes. He reinvents geometry with bits of colored cloth when he's three years old and then reinvents all mathematics and finally asks somebody how long it will be for a line pointed straight up to come back from underneath to where it started. You see, that's relativity."

"Is it?"

"Oh sure. Einstein said space is curved."

"That does seem precocious to figure out all by yourself. What finally happens to this boy?"

"As I said, it's very surprising. He turns into a cretin. He just sits down and won't move or look at anything and at the very end of the story his mother is overjoyed because he's learned to hold a fork and put a bite of food in his mouth."

"Like the line that comes back on itself from underneath."

"I hadn't thought of that."

"Please stop reading those stories," Peggy said from within her drying hair. "They can't be good for your psyche."

"That's what I used to tell Joey," my mother called, "and he never paid the slightest attention."

"And look how healthy my psyche is!" I called back to her.

"Ha ha," Peggy said.

Soon, sooner than we had expected, my mother had set the meal on the table: the peas, and boiled potatoes flecked with parsley, and, cold from the Armour's can, a pressed ham she asked me to slice. The knife startled me by being sharp. My father had cared about knives and tools, and might have made a good craftsman had he not been expected, like me, to work with intangibles. When I had served everybody, my mother asked Richard what he would like to do in life.

"How do you mean exactly?"

"Do you want to live in New York and do what Joey does, whatever it is? I've never understood it; he won't explain it to me."

I had explained it to her many times. I work for a firm which arranges educational programs for corporations on such matters as tax minimization, overseas expansion, federal contract acquisition, and automation. My specialty is advertising dollar distribution, which is to say, broadly, corporate image presentation. My mother had wanted me to be a poet, like Wordsworth. She rarely read poetry but had a clear dogmatic sense of its importance. I had been sent, over my father's pleas for an engineering school, to Harvard, because Harvard had graduated, from Emerson to Eliot, more poets than any other American college. The pleasant joke on my father was that I graduated into a world where a flexible student of old fables could soon earn more, in the widening multicentered, public-relations-minded affluence, than all but a few engineers. I do not know when, if ever, I gave up my poetic ambitions. I think I married Joan because, when I first saw her wheeling her bicycle through the autumnal dusk of the Yard, she suggested, remote and lithe and inward, the girl of "The Solitary Reaper" and, close-up, seemed a half-hidden Lucy who might make "oh, the difference to me!"

"His father," Peggy said, "is an academic."

"You mean a scholar?" My mother didn't wait to be answered, continuing firmly, "Richard shows scholarly tastes. He reminds me of myself at his age, except that I read all the time because reality seemed too painful—that's not how it is with you, is it, Richard?"

"Not painful so much as boring," he said.

"Well I don't wonder," my mother said, "living in that air-conditioned city where the seasons are all the same. Here on my farm every week is different, every day is a surprise. New faces in the fields, the birds say different things, and nothing repeats. Nature never repeats; this August evening has never been before and it will never be again."

She was indulging herself in sadness, so I cut in with what was in some sense a joke. I asked her, "Do you think Richard should be a poet?"

She said, "No, I've thought that about one boy and I try not to repeat myself. The world is so different now. There are so few jobs that seem to *do* anything."

"I could be a selenographer," the boy said.

"What's that?" my mother asked, moving her hands carefully around her food, too aware of the possibility that she was being ridiculed.

"A moon-geographer," Richard explained. "They're going to need people on the moon who can make maps."

"You can specialize in the dark side," I said.

"That's where they're going to put a great telescope," he told us. "You know why?"

"Why?" Peggy asked, after a pause.

"Because on the side toward us there will be too much earthshine. Earthshine," he told my mother, "is like moonshine only the other way around. It's blue."

She did not respond, and I knew, knew on my prickling skin, that she had clouded, having felt, in our digression away from her earth, a personal affront.

I asked, "Isn't that side too cold?"

Richard said, "Not if you dig down below the surface. Fifty feet down or so the moon is a uniform temperature, about ten degrees centigrade."

My mother was actually taking his interest in the moon as a personal desertion. She hunched motionless above her plate, the wings of her nostrils white, her breathing frozen.

Peggy felt the strangeness and said, to be polite, "Do you think Richard should be a farmer?"

My mother lifted her large head. Her forehead was mottled. "I think it would take more imagination, Peggy, than you'll permit him to have."

Shocked, I interceded, "Why, I think she lets him have *lots* of imagination. He's America's youngest m-moon-mapper." In my haste my tongue had jammed and I stuttered.

Peggy's hands pressed back her hair tight against her small skull. "I can't imagine what you mean." Her voice was fluting and thrilling and phony—a model's voice. Off and on since her divorce, she had modelled for fashion showings, but never for photographs; her figure was too wide, and her bony fighter's face showed up on film as asymmetric.

"I'm sorry, Peggy, you're trying hard but so are we all. You should not be jealous of me and this boy."

"Jealous? You're fantastic."

My mother turned to me, as if to her historian, and said, "She takes my grandchildren from me, she turns my son into a gray-haired namby-pamby, and now she won't let me show this poor worried child a little affection, which he badly needs."

"He receives lots of affection," Peggy said.

"Oh, I'm sure you do what the doctor tells you. I mean something less mechanical."

"I've kept him sound for five years without a father."

"Well, why did he lack a father in the first place?"

"I could explain it to you, but you wouldn't listen."

My mother shrugged. "You'd be surprised, the things I've

listened to." She was calm, I realized, unclouded; her outburst had cleared her.

I became afraid for Peggy, afraid she would misjudge, trip and fall. Her speed, the speed of her youth, was her safety; this quarrel still had a surface, upon which she must skim. "As to Joey and me," she said, "I'm the first woman he's ever met who was willing to let him be a man." This was her secret song, the justification with which she had led me into divorce.

"Maybe," my mother said, "we mean different things by the word 'man.'"

"I'm sure we do, if what you did to your husband is an example of what you mean."

My mother turned to me and said, "Poor Joan had ideas as to how I should do my wash, but at least she never offered to revise my marriage for me."

"You ask for it, Mother," I told her, angry because Peggy had suddenly lost momentum and sunk. Her eyes sank into tears and her face sank into her hands; her fingers blindly clasped her temples and her hair fell forward as if before the fire.

Again she was displayed; again, as last night, my mother's gaze touched her and returned to me offended. "What do I ask for?"

"You ask for advice, for pity. You carry yourself as if you've made a terrible mistake. You pretend you emasculated Daddy and when some innocent soul offers to agree with you you're hurt."

Richard asked, "What's emasculated?" He had taken upon himself my dinner-table chore of jesting, of using his voice in the hope of breaking a grim rhythm.

"It's what mules are," I told him.

My mother laughed. "He *was* mulish," she said, and her sodden bent frame lightened, as if this animal analogy had solved one of the last remaining riddles of her life.

Peggy lifted her face, soft and shy in its blurred veil of tears. "How can you laugh?"

My mother said, "How can you cry? All I was asking you was why your son couldn't touch my tractor."

"Mother, he *did* touch it."

"There are four forward gears," he said, "and one pedal engages the clutch, and the other engages the shaft that makes the cutter blade whirl around."

"Peggy," my mother said, "I can see we'll have to have a talk about our husbands. But later. I'm afraid we'll ruin Richard's appetite."

"Is there any more," he asked, "of that molasses pie?"

"Shoo-fly," I said.

"You didn't like it last night," my mother told him.

Peggy sniffled, and said, "I thought it was butterfly pie," and insniffed prolongedly, a pleased comedienne, as we all laughed, loving her. Or so I imagined: I have always had difficulty believing that anyone could look at Peggy and not love her, which has made my calculations concerning her inexact. It is possible that I could have retained her, as mistress, as long as her beauty lasted, while remaining married to Joan. But I was prey to jealous fantasies and felt the world to be full of resolute men who, if they once glimpsed her long legs groping with half-bared thighs from a taxicab, would carry her off forever.

The air of the house had taken a wound. Though the rain beat sweetly around us, urging us to unite at the fire that had dwindled to the purity of its embers, there were distances that did not close, an atmospheric soreness that pressed on my ears with a fine high ringing. The lurching of the tractor had settled into my muscles so that my bones seemed encrusted with stale motion and gave me, as I sat reading an old Wodehouse novel that was lifeless, an illusion of swaying.

"Joey, the fire is hungry. Could you possibly run down into the cellar?"

These were the first words my mother had spoken since

dinner. She did the dishes while Peggy and Richard played Parcheesi on the living-room rug. They had found an old warped board in a cupboard, and an imperfect set of counters they pieced out with buttons and pennies. While reading, I wanted to hush the rattle of the dice and the click of the counters and their excited yips and groans; my mother's sullen clattering in the kitchen seemed a monologue I must listen to instead. It was a relief to hear her speak.

I had forgotten the cellar: dried paint cans, turpentine, apples, Mason jars bearded with spider cocoons, potatoes dumbly odorous of earth in a bin against which split logs fragrant of the winter woods had been stacked by my dead father, a glistening hill of coal, a squat furnace branching into aluminum ducts overspreading the cellar ceiling. Once my father and I had spent a hellish afternoon down here tugging stiffening cement this way and that across the dirt. I noticed with surprise that the floor we had made that day was smooth and level and innocent of seepage; it was as if the day itself were preserved, an underground pond, a lake of treasure in a vault.

I carried up the wood and fed the fire. The dogs, all three of them, had been let into the house by my mother and lay in a long damp heap on the sofa, asleep. One bright round eye opened when I dumped the wood on the andirons, and an animal wheezed. Peggy did not look up from her game, though the resurgent glow described the curve of her thighs. Before dinner she had gone upstairs and changed from her slip into a cashmere sweater and the smoky-blue stretch pants that imitate dungarees. I wiped the crumbs of bark from my hands and went back into my book. A strange stealth had been imposed on us. The rain lowered its voice. Richard whispered something to Peggy drowned out for me by the rustle of a page as I turned it.

In the kitchen, my mother smashed a plate. To abolish any

doubt that it had been deliberate, she smashed another, after a bleached space of dumbfounded silence; the explosion was somewhat muddier than the first, as if the plate had struck the floor diagonally.

The heap of fur on the sofa stirred and churned itself into three individual dogs. The biggest, ears erect, bristled, leaped onto a windowsill, and began barking at an imagined attacker. The smallest, the puppy, scurried into the kitchen, its pale tail-tip wagging low, undecided between fear and amusement. We followed the dog into the kitchen. My mother was holding in her two hands, chest high, a third dish, an oval blue platter, and clearly, having hesitated, had passed the moment when she could have smashed it also. It was the platter of the set she had received at the Olinger movie house, Tuesday after Tuesday, before the war. Putting it down on the table, she cried with a semblance of agony, "What's all the whispering!"

Alone on the cleared table was a white china sugar bowl I had sent on some anniversary from San Francisco. Peggy snatched it up, asked, "Is this a new game?," and dropped it to the floor. The bowl bounced without breaking, tossing its sugar upward in an hallucinatory figure eight, like a twist of smoke, then complacently rolled to the baseboard, bumping on its handles.

I asked my mother, "What whispering?"

"You were whispering. I heard Richard whispering."

"He was asking me why it was so quiet," Peggy said.

"Well why *is* it?"

"You know damn well why," Peggy said. "You're throwing a sulk and worrying your son."

"My son? My son worries me. He says I killed his father."

I said, "I never said that." My mother's face, turning to me, seemed vast, as the slanting veined faces of rocks in tidewater look vast, wet and stricken, between waves.

"I'm tired," she said, "of being hated. I've lost everything but this child's respect and I don't want him whispering."

"Nobody hates you."

"Well *I'm* tired," Peggy said, "of *this*," and she glanced around so that we could see how in her eyes our house was a maze. "I'm not going to keep Richard exposed to so much neuroticism. Joey, you can drive us back or come later on your own. I'm sorry, Mrs. Robinson, but I don't feel I'm a help here and we'll both feel better if I go."

"It's night," I said.

She told me, "Stay or come, it's up to you. I lived alone five years and unlike some men I'm not afraid of the dark."

"Bravo," I said. *"Die Königin der Nacht."*

"Sweetie, I'm packing." Peggy went upstairs. The stair door latch resisted and—legs spread, backside broadened— she tore it open vehemently.

"She *has* been a help," my mother said in a small mild voice. Hysteria fell from her like a pose.

"I'll go talk to her." Richard's voice cracked between assumed gravity and a child's alto.

"What'll you say?" I wanted to go to her myself and was jealous. More precisely, I wanted to be his size and to go to her.

"I don't know, but I'll think of something." His smile showed the gap between his teeth. "I'm very good at calming her down."

"Tell her," my mother called, as the boy went up the staircase, "that I've been meaning to throw away those old blue plates for a long time." To me she added, "Never liked them anyway, but they were free. Silly what greed makes you do."

"Let's smash," I said, "all the pictures of me you have sitting around."

"Don't you touch them. Those pictures are my son. Those pictures are the only son I have."

"You have such dramatic ideas, Mother."

In an attitude of weariness so little exaggerated that it left her the option to smile or not, I took the dustpan and brush from behind the refrigerator and swept up the shards of blue plate and grains of white sugar. The puppy tried to help and his solicitous moist nose kept jostling my hand. When I straightened up, my mother, finishing her drying, flirted her head at the silent ceiling and said, topping my mythological allusion, "Cupid interviewing Venus."

I said, "If Joan had ever offered to pack I might still be married to her."

"I can't imagine why you blame me for Joan," she said.

"What do I blame on you, the marriage or the divorce?"

"Both. Your father was like that. Women made the rules, women made the babies, women did everything. He used to say he had no recollection of asking me to marry him, it was just something I'd made happen."

The contents of the dustpan slithered, *slash*, into the wastebasket, a cheap battered thing painted on each side with bouquets of red roses tied with gold ribbon. My father had salvaged it from the stage set of a high school play. Like many of my father's fragile redemptions, it had absurdly endured. "Poor Charlie," I said. "I wonder now if he'll become like Richard, a little husband."

"Poor Charlie, yes. How could you have done it, Joey?"

"It seemed necessary. Charlie still knows he's my son."

I had remained staring into the wastebasket, seeking in its jagged contents perhaps some revelation as to the state of my abandoned son's mind, so I was taken unawares when my mother, moving behind me, put her hand on the back of my skull, just above the neck. "Such a lot of sadness," she said, "in such a little head."

Footsteps sounded on the stairs; we pulled apart guiltily. Richard came into the kitchen and proudly told us, "She'll stay."

I asked him, "What did you say to her?"

"I said it would be impolite."

"You're a genius. That would never have occurred to me."

My mother asked him, "What would you like for a reward?"

The boy pointed at me. "He says you have some nature books that tell the names of plants. Could I look at them, please?"

"Plants. You don't want birds."

"I think I should begin with plants."

"All I have that I can remember is an old Schuyler Mathews *Wild Flowers* with crinkly pages. I got it when I was in normal school and I used to go out into the fields with a paint box and try to tint the drawings to match. I think it's still on the shelf if the silver fish haven't eaten it."

"I'll be careful with it."

"What plant in particular interests you?"

"Oh, none in particular. I thought I could begin in the beginning and read through. I'm a fast reader. Then I'll know them all."

My mother smiled. "I'm not sure that will work," she said. "You don't know the plants until you see them really, and most of them in the book you'll never see at all, unless you become a botanist. Or a hobo."

"Along the lake where I went camping once there were *oodles* of a bright purple thing."

"I don't know what that was," my mother said. "I've never lived near the water. The purplest thing around here is joe-pye weed. We can look *him* up and see if he has any relatives. Come to think of it, the book had a color index."

They went into the living room. I went upstairs to Peggy. The bedrooms were empty. I called, and she rapped within the bathroom. When she came out, she was annoyed at having been disturbed. In one hand she held a small object wrapped around with toilet paper through which blood was seeping. "What do I do with this?" she asked, and frowned. Her sunburned eye sockets and cheekbones looked rouged, like those of an oriental actress.

"I'll take it," I said, extending my hand, "and treasure it religiously."

"No." She was not amused and refused to look directly at me; her eyes examined the corners of the room. "There's no wastebasket anywhere."

"There's one downstairs."

"Your mother will see it."

"And use it for voodoo. God, I'm sorry."

"For what now?"

"For that scene."

"It wasn't so bad. I thought both she and I were trying to keep from laughing."

I laughed. "I don't know what goes on in her mind."

"It's very clear. She wants a man to be on this farm and thinks she's lost you."

"But she never had me. I never liked the farm."

"Oh, I think you do like it. You like it the same way you like me. It's something big you can show off."

I was touched by this humble conception of herself, so dis-illusioned and so nearly true. "It's your fault," I said, "for be-ing worth showing off." She crossed to our bureau and put the used Tampax in her pocketbook. "You're angry," I said.

"Please get out of my way. I'm going downstairs."

"Don't smash anything."

"I'm going to do just what you told me. I'm going to be myself."

"Wait. Peggy. Thanks for not leaving."

"I wouldn't possibly leave you here."

"I would have gone with you."

"I wouldn't do that to your mother. Why don't you try to think of what it's like for her in her position instead of taking every move she makes as a threat?"

"The threat is to you."

At last she looked directly at me; one hand smoothed back her hair. "Why are you hostile?" She answered herself. "You wanted me to go."

"God, no; don't leave me, woman!" My plaint was comic.

Peggy smiled and said, "The cute thing about you, Joey, is you're really sort of a bastard." She passed me dismissingly as the overhead light at the head of the stairs struck her skin. Of her skin: my wife's skin blanches when she is angry, grows very smooth in making love, and takes a tan briefly, as if the atoms composing it dance with especial rapidity. Her forearms are freckled and downy in a way that coltishly prolongs their length; her heels are yellow and tough from the bite of fashionable shoes; her belly is so white the bluish stretchmarks seem to vein marble. Where her skin redly shows wear and age I yearn to lean and lift with kisses the burden of use endured, I somehow imagine, since her birth for my sake. There is a tone that is for me the tone of life and it lies on her skin, or closely under it, as a diffused light. As she passed beneath the overhead light a parabolic shadow leaped down from her brows and her profile told sharply against the whitewashed plaster of the outer stair wall. I followed her down.

My mother and Richard were on the sofa beside the dogs, bent above a weather-beaten little book with wavy pages. "Bindweed," my mother was saying, "more commonly around here called morning glory. A field full of morning glories makes farmers very sad. It shows tired soil."

"It says here convo—convolulus."

"The Latin names are wonderful." She turned the page and read, "Phlox pilosa. Phlox divaricata. Phlox subulata. Some people call phlox pinks."

"I've often wondered why flowers are never green. Except around Saint Patrick's Day when they have these green carnations."

"They wouldn't be noticed. The bees couldn't see them in the leaves. The whole point of flowers is to attract the bees. Flowers are bright for the same reason your mother wears such pretty clothes." Only by this remark did she acknowledge that we had come into the room. I returned to the Wodehouse and Peggy picked up the Parcheesi pieces. The fire was comfortably low. The rain had settled into a drumming steadiness. The two bigger dogs begged to go out. My mother and Richard took them with a pan of dogfood to the pen and when they came in with wet shoulders from the dark Peggy told the boy it was time for him to go to bed. She asked me to take him up, though I had reached a section of the novel, involving the theft of a prize pig, that seemed genuinely funny. But I obeyed.

Once Richard had been shy about my seeing him undressed. Now he thoughtlessly removed under my eyes his T-shirt saying YALE, the tattered sneakers he wore without socks, the khaki shorts Peggy had thriftily cut from worn-out suntans, his elastic underpants. His taut buttocks had a pearly pallor; his thin-edged shoulders were nut-brown. Naked, he seemed a faun, incongruous in this low-ceilinged room of rigidly repeated flowers. He showed me, on his legs and belly, where he had been scratched when Grammy showed him where the blackberries were.

"Grammy?"

"Your mother. That's what she told me to call her."

"Good idea. Your pajamas are under the pillow."

"I should have brought up the flower book to read."

"Brush your teeth first."

"Oh, I couldn't forget to do *that*, that would be sacrilegious. Mother would have a fit."

"You'll be grateful. I've had terrible teeth, and it's been a big nuisance."

"Didn't you brush them?"

"When I thought of it. The real problem was, I ate too much shoo-fly pie." I had turned away, to look again at the photograph of Joan. She seemed engaged in some vigil, her eyes uplifted, her arm glowing; and it seemed unlikely that her hope, whatever it was, would be rewarded here in this old lonely farmhouse.

"Hey." Richard still had no name for me.

"Yes, my lad?" I was conscious of courting him.

"Why did your mother smash those plates?"

"I guess she thought they had outlived their usefulness, I don't know."

"No, really. Was she mad at my mother for wearing her bathing suit?"

He was eleven. I tried to remember how much I knew at eleven. At about that age I came home from a birthday party where we had played Spin-the-bottle, and my mother, per- haps with an irony I didn't grasp, had behaved as if I had been ravished, assaulted—as if the lipstick on my mouth were blood. "I don't think she would be mad about that. Why should she mind your mother's being a flower?"

"The odd fact is, a bee did almost sting her."

"Your mother?"

"Up in the field. I told her to stand very still and, sure enough, eventually it flew away."

"You're a good protector of your mother." He was listening but heard no irony. I went on, "I think the reason *my* mother smashed the dishes was to remind us that she was *there*. She's afraid we'll forget her. It's a fear people have when they're her age."

"She doesn't seem so old."

"She does to me. I knew her when she was just like your mother."

"In what way?"

"In being young. When we lived in another house, in a town, she used to run to catch the trolley car. Once I had a balsa-wood airplane get stuck in a tree and she climbed the tree for me. She used to be very athletic. In college she was on the hockey varsity."

"My mother is worthless at sports. My father couldn't stand to play tennis with her."

I seemed to be in bed, and a tall girl stood above me, and her hair came loose from her shoulder and fell forward with a swift liquid motion, and hung there, as a wing edged with light, and enclosed me in a kind of tent as she bent lower to deliver her good-night kiss. It was to this that my trying to remember my mother as young and slim had brought me. There was a sense of, beyond my tall window, a vacant lot where the older children of the neighborhood were still playing. I said to Richard, "Let's brush your teeth."

I watched him brush, admiring his brisk method, thinking of all the small tasks whose mastery goes into making an adult. He spat in the basin, rinsed his brush with fascinating thoroughness, and turned, showing me a minty grimace that became, as a joke, a lion's snarl. Nothing is more surprising in children than the way, less out of an ignorance of danger than by virtue of their simple animal freshness, they give us the courage we need to defend them. The black and murmuring window behind him mirrored the back of his head as if a hairy monster were peering in. The entire warm wet night seemed a siege of our lit position. As I stood guard, he urinated solemnly, his pelvis thrust forward to enlarge the margin for error, his long-lashed eyes ritually attending the mixing of waters. This, too, I realized, remembering a little bench I had built for Charlie so he could stand up to the bowl like a man, is a skill that must be mastered.

I offered to read Richard a story. He seemed amused. "I can read faster to myself."

"I know. I thought you might find it soothing. I guess I miss having children I can read to."

"O.K. You can read to me. Shall I go down and get the flower book?"

"I think that would make terrible reading aloud."

"There's the science-fiction anthology."

"Your mother doesn't think those are good bedtime stories."

"She's full of needless anxieties."

"I'll tell you what. Let me tell you a story."

"Can you?"

"I used to tell one every night. The children were"—I was going to say "mine"—"smaller; so you'll have to pardon me if the age-level seems wrong."

"That's O.K. I enjoy childish things."

I wondered if he realized he was echoing the Bible. His mother now and then used the word "know" in the, I had thought, obsolete Biblical sense. *I didn't know a man until I was nineteen. Of course, Joey, it's always better for the woman after she knows the man.* Their unthinking non-Christianity sometimes worried me, and I blamed myself for having never gathered the nerve to teach Richard a good-night prayer, as I had done with my own children. I closed my eyes, and felt him, as one star feels the tug of another in the blindness of space, close his also.

"Once," I began, "there was a frog in the rain. The rain beat"—I groped outward through my senses for an image—"on his warty skin like on a roof, and he was very pleased to have such a watertight skin."

"All skin is watertight."

I opened my eyes, saw that his were staring at my face with that gleam of impudence or wariness I remembered on the face of his father, and doubted that he had ever closed them.

"His," I said, "felt especially so, because he was so small inside it."

"How do you mean? That doesn't make sense."

"He was like a tiny king inside his castle inside his body. When he gave a command, huge legs catapulted him from one lily pad to the next, and when he gave another command a tongue like a crossbow on a string flew through the air and speared a poor fly." How many times had I heard lately the phrase "poor Joan"? "This frog," I said, "felt his mouth to be as great as a drawgate, and his eyes were on the tip-top of his head like turrets, and he had heard rumors of a wonderful treasure stored deep in the dungeon of his guts, where he had never been."

"Guts." Richard laughed.

Downstairs, Peggy and my mother began to talk. I could not make out the words. I hastened to complete my story.

"Well," I said, "one day, when the rain had stopped and leaves were falling, and things were turning brown, the frog got bored and decided to go and find this wonderful treasure that someone, he didn't know who, had told him was there. So he went down a circular staircase out of his head—"

Richard laughed; I wondered if braces would be required by the gap between his teeth and decided that Peggy and the dentist must have discussed it.

"—down through the great barrel of his throat, the curving ladder of his ribs, through a gloomy vaulted room where his footsteps echoed—"

"This is like Doctor Seuss," Richard said.

"I mean it to be like Dante," I said. "You've heard of Dante?"

"He sounds French."

"Close. Down and down, into stranger and darker rooms, and the lower he went, the smaller he got, until finally, just when he was sure he had reached the dungeon where the treasure was, he disappeared!"

The boy's eyes widened in the silence, so I could observe, dissected in the lamplight, the layers of color—granular, radial, delicately torn-looking—held within his brown irises. The voices of the women under us were rising; I listened in vain for laughter.

"Is that the end?" Richard asked. "He died?"

"Who said he died? He just became so small he couldn't find himself. He was hibernating."

"Oh. That's right. You said the leaves were falling."

"You really think death is disappearing?"

"I don't know."

"Good. I don't either. Anyway, after a while, in the spring, the frog woke up, looked around in the darkness, ran up through the rooms, up the circular stairs, to his eyes, threw open the lids, and looked out. And the sky was blue. End of story."

"I like the idea of throwing open the lids."

"Thank you. You were very good to listen."

"Will you ever tell me another?"

"Probably not. You're too old."

"How old is Charlie now?"

"Charlie?"

"Your real son."

"He's seven now. Eight in October."

"That's not too young for me to play with."

"You don't think so? We'll have to arrange it. He'll be back in New York pretty soon."

"I know." Peggy had told him. I felt Peggy behind his polite interest. Unlike her, I was not yet able to picture an uncatastrophic state of things, when the stepchildren could play together as if divorce were a mode of cousinage.

"Shall I get you a book now to read yourself? Which, the flowers or science fiction?"

"Skip it, I'm pretty pooped. I think I'll just lie here and listen to the rain. Last night I heard an owl hoot."

"So did I. I'll turn this lamp off but leave the light in the bathroom on."

"You don't have to. I'm not afraid of the dark."

"I don't want you to wake up and not know where you are." Bending to switch off the light, I continued the motion and attempted to kiss him. Though it was unusual, he expected it, and turned his head in the rigid wriggly way boys have, whether toward me or away was unclear in the dark. My lips fell on the creased space of skin just beside one corner of his mouth.

"O.K., frog," I said.

Going downstairs, toward the voices that were growing in the light, I was touched, enclosed, by a faint familiar tint of vapor, that I assumed a moment's hesitation would reveal to be some nostalgic treasure unlocked by the humidity within the stones, plaster, wood, and history of the house. But in fact the presence, rising from a damp towel tossed onto the landing, was the hoarse scent of Peggy's wet hair.

———

MY WIFE and my mother talked, talked from eight-thirty to ten, and though their conversation—in which eddies of disagreement nonsensically dissolved as one or the other left the room and returned with a refilled glass of wine or a handful of pretzels or a weak gin-and-tonic, and where suffocating tunnels of tension broke onto plateaus of almost idyllic reminiscence that imperceptibly narrowed again—was in a sense the climax and purpose of our visit, I could not quite listen. While they talked, my mother half-lying on the sofa soaked in dog hair and Peggy leaning forward from within the wing chair where my grandfather had pontificated, I sat between them, on the blue-painted lawn chair, reading Wodehouse. Occasionally I would be addressed, appealed to:

"Did you feel your father, Joey, was so put upon? Where did this girl get the idea if not from you?"

"You've told me yourself, Joey, you weren't allowed to have dates until you were eighteen."

"Joey, is it true Joan was unfaithful, or is this what they call projection?"

"Joey, stand by me! If you're silent now you must have lied to me before."

"Does she always take such a lofty tone, Joey, or is it looking at me that makes her hysterical?"

In the stretches between these urgently darted hooks, which would snap up my head painfully and drag from me words of placation, self-defense, or impatience, I was conscious—while in my lap some transparent eccentrics cavorted through a landscape purely green—of an onflowing voluminous conversation in whose murk two exasperatingly clumsy spirits were passing, searching for, and repassing one another; deeper and deeper their voices dived into the darkness that was each woman to the other, in pursuit of shadows that I supposed were my father and myself. Peggy's idea, which now, in the awful fullness of this exchange, she could expand from a suspicion to an accusation, a detailed indictment of a past that had touched her only through my hands, was that my mother had undervalued and destroyed my father, had been inadequately a "woman" to him, had brought him to a farm which was in fact her giant lover, and had thus warped the sense of the masculine within me, her son. Overhearing her dimly, I thought of my father as he had been, in his stubborn corporeality, his comic kindness— he indulged himself in self-denial as other men are sensualists— and closed my mind against her voice, so painfully did it fail to harmonize with the simple, inexpressible way that things had been. And my mother, on her side, swept forward with a fabulous counter-system of which I was the center, the only child, the obscurely chosen, the poet, raped, ignorantly, from my ideally immaterial and unresisting wife and hurled into the shidepoke sin of adultery and the eternal curse of my children's fatherlessness. "Look at his eyes!" my mother shockingly cried, and I looked up, giving them, in my face, the evidence both sought.

Perhaps they were both right. All misconceptions are themselves data which have the minimal truth of existing in at least one mind. Truth, my work had taught me, is not something static, a mountain-top that statements approximate like successive assaults of frostbitten climbers. Rather, truth is constantly being formed from the solidification of illusions. In New York I work among men whose fallacies are next year worn everywhere, like the new style of shoes.

Out of fear I refused to listen to my wife and mother. Their sweeping disruption of the past threatened to show me that I had never known my father and was a blank to myself. Their conversation seemed a collision of darknesses to me but my mother's darkness was nurturing whereas Peggy's was cold, dense, and metallic. Surely in becoming my wife she had undertaken, with me, the burden of mothering my mother, of accommodating herself to the warps of that enclosing spirit. Her cigarette smoke insulted the room.

The puppy shifted from the sofa to the hearth rug, once a bathmat, and from there, troubled by the combustion near his ears, transferred himself to the kitchen and the space beneath the dining table. The fire needed fresh wood. I went into the cellar, where my father's ghost still labored, and returned with my arms full. The fire reawakened, and I thought that to its wild gaze Peggy, proud and stiff in her wing chair, must seem as inflexibly in profile as a playing card. Parallel to the rain's infiltrating murmur, my mother was telling her, "I used to worry about Joey. He had this cruel streak. He never tortured insects but he would torment his toys. We could hear him in his room, talking to them, trying to make them confess. His father thought it was the effect of war propaganda. It might have been. I thought it might be more the case that pain was too real to him, so he was fascinated by it. When we first moved to the farm we got a puppy for him, Mitzi. He would tease her so badly she would hide in the drainpipe down by the chicken shed. But she was growing, and one day she was too big to turn around in there and come out. Joey came running to me; I've never seen such an expression on a face, and I remember thinking at the time, that no matter what happens to him, he'll never go through anything worse. He had tried to dig down to the buried end of the pipe with his bare hands. Actually, by the time we got down, the dog had come to the conclusion that she must back out. Dogs are remarkably acute animals. A horse would never have made such a deduction. I've heard of horses burning to death with an open door right behind them. When I was a little girl, in Alton for market day, I saw a horse strangle itself trying to run with a buggy whose axle had snapped. At any rate, what I didn't like about this incident with Mitzi is that Joey was terribly grateful to the dog for saving herself, but whenever he felt a bit mean he would take her down there and show her the hole and pretend to put her in the pipe again. I thought that was ungentlemanly."

The rain and my mother's voice had merged for Peggy; at the point where they intersected, she nodded once, twice, and fell asleep. In a moment she stood up, all dignity, and said, "Excuse me. I think I should go to bed."

My mother said, "That's a smart idea, Peggy. I've enjoyed our talk, though I'm not sure I've explained myself."

"I don't think one ever can," Peggy said; her dip into sleep had blurred her face. She turned, smiled down at me as if I were an interloper to whom she should be polite, and left without giving me an opportunity to go with her.

My mother said, when the footsteps on the floor above our heads had gone into the bathroom and ceased, "Do you think you've made a mistake?"

"A mistake how?"

"By divorcing Joan and marrying Peggy." I was pleased that she should call my wife by her name so simply, and in precisely the same tone with which she pronounced "Joan." She might have been speaking of two daughters.

"Yes, yes. Yes."

"Yes what?" She smiled apologetically at our difficulty in comprehending one another.

"Yes, it was wrong."

Her eyebrows lifted, perhaps at my rewording her question. Her words seemed snipped from another line of thought. "The children?"

"Wrong even leaving them out of account. Joan did not make me happy, especially, but she was what my life had been directed to go through. In leaving her I put my life out of joint."

"And other lives."

"It's hard to move without touching other lives."

"That's what I said to myself when we bought the farm."

I said, "I knew it was a mistake even before it was too late to change." I spoke with a voice that—slightly plangent and quick—did not seem mine, though it arose within me. "But it had gone so far that, I guess it was Daddy's stubbornness, I was damned if I'd back out."

"More like Daddy's curiosity."

"That's it; I had to see what it would be like."

"What is it like?"

"Wonderful, really. But there are moments when she seems to be a blank wall. She can be terribly obtuse."

"She's not subtle."

"Not as subtle as us, no."

"Not as subtle as Joan."

"Why did you dislike Joan so much? In the end you made me dislike her."

"You imagine that. I liked Joan. She had a style. She had what they used to call poise. It's very rare. She reminded me of Daddy's sister, and I was always a little uncomfortable with my sister-in-law, was all. I felt when I got too near her that I hadn't quite washed everywhere. It was you who didn't like Joan."

"I didn't *know* her, would be more exact."

"Yes. In a way, Joan snubbed you."

"I love her now. It's amazing, how much I love her, now that she's in Canada."

"With Joan, you still had the space to be a poet. That's who you love, the poet you can never become now."

"Poet. It was you who wanted to be the poet."

"No. I wanted to be a farmer. My father, who was a farmer, wanted to be an orator."

I laughed at the ease with which she, short of breath and recumbent, could weave these patterns. "And now," I said, "you've become the orator and me the farmer."

She shifted her position with a small cry, as of soft pain. "Oh, don't laugh, Joey. How can you laugh when you've brought my death into the house?"

"How?"

"That woman. She's fierce. She'll have me dead within the year."

"You think?"

"You watch. I saw my mother put Grammy Hofstetter away without laying a finger on her. When I saw her trip so gaily down the walk last night I knew I was kissing my own death."

"Mother, you're too egocentric. She doesn't know you. She doesn't *care* about you and your farm."

"Don't you believe it. She's from Nebraska and knows a good piece of land when she sees it. She wants the money sitting in these acres. You should have seen her perk up as we walked along the upper road where the first lots would be."

I laughed, since I could picture it; Peggy is a passionate window shopper.

My mother went on, "You may make more money than your father but you don't make enough to support two women. Don't think she and Joan are going to eat peaceably out of the same dish. Joey, you've bought an expensive piece of property. These cute little Iwo Jimas or whatever they are and Lord and

Taylor pants and transparent nighties aren't bought with just wishing."

"Her nighties aren't transparent."

"No, but her eyes are and I see my son's ruin in them."

Perhaps it was merely that, feeling my mother's fright at her coming death, I needed a great grief of my own as an answer, an exchange; but there seemed truth in what she said. *Ruin*. It pleased me to feel myself sinking, smothered, lost, forgotten, obliterated in the depths of the mistake which my mother, as if enrolling my fall in her mythology, enunciated:

"You've taken a vulgar woman to be your wife."

It was true.

She shrugged, and said, speaking less to me than into the record, the weave of truth that needs perpetual adjusting, "Well, the Bible tells us we all waste our patrimony. The wonder is, after six thousand years, there's anything left in the world to waste."

"She *is* simple-minded." I am always a little behind my mother, always arriving at the point from which she has departed. She smiled, seeing me sitting upright, excited like a boy by my discovery of the obvious. "She sees with one eye."

"Well you knew that."

"No," I said. "I threw myself into her. I gave her credit for everything I thought. I couldn't believe that anything so beautiful could be less intelligent than I. I must have thought she had made herself."

"See, you forgot God."

My mother's wantonness is most conspicuous here; her religiosity comes and goes as beckoned. "Actually," I said, wishing to curve my words precisely around the sore area her accusation had touched, "I've never felt so serene about that. I find that's one consolation of being middle-aged. Or of having a loving wife." I think I meant that I believed.

With the curious abrupt impatience that, like the lightness

of her voice, had come to live on the edges of her inert mass and central incapacity, she waved Peggy and God away. "Now what about the farm?"

"What about it? It exists."

"Is it going to vanish when I do?"

I got up from the chair, somehow offended; my emotion, if it could be fitted to a sin, was one of jealousy. "I scarcely think," I told my mother, "you're on the point of vanishing." I was angry at the ease with which she had accepted my betrayal of Peggy, had absorbed it parasitically, sitting there motionless, devoting her thought, her innermost thought, not to me but to her farm. So I scorned her death.

"It's almost on me, Joey!" Her voice was warped, urgent, and diminished, and from her position on the sofa there did seem something pressing her down, bending her face backwards so the soft pale neck was bared. My throat engorged, as if I had surprised my parents in coitus. I wanted to flee, but some thread—the courtesy of estrangement, a child's habit of waiting for permission—held me fast, amid the walls of rain and photographs, between the dark kitchen and the fire collapsing into its ashes.

My mother looked at me alertly. By one of those sharp withdrawals by which she kept me, in the end, at a son's distance, she sat up and said, "I hope all that work wasn't too much for you today."

I said, "I feel pleasantly stiff."

She said, "Your eyes have that puffy look they used to get in goldenrod season. I thought living by the sea had cured you."

I said, "I'm sorry more didn't get done. If you'd let me, I could probably do at least the small field tomorrow before we go."

She asked, "When must you go?"

"By the middle of the afternoon at the latest. Monday's a work day and a school day for Richard."

She sighed, "We'll see. Now don't keep Peggy waiting any longer."

"Do you want to use the bathroom first?"

"No, you go."

"Pleasant dreams."

"Pleasant dreams."

In the staircase the rain had a different voice, and at the head of the steps its pattering seemed trapped on the wrong side of the window and to be searching among the dry magazines stacked, untouched since my father's death, on the deep sill. Richard's breath skipped a beat and I stood a moment, satisfying myself that he was asleep. I entered our bedroom timidly. Its darkness, wrapped around with rain, was complete, save for a glimmer left lingering in the mirror above the bureau. Rather than risk waking Peggy in searching for my pajamas, I crept into bed in my underpants. The space receiving me seemed enormous. My foot stealthily travelled a wide arc before encountering Peggy's still skin. She was on her back. The window on my side had been left open a crack; the drumming of the rain was delicately amplified, fanned into a rainbow of sound, by this prism of air. Cool spray grazed my face, my hand beside my face, my naked chest. I sneezed. All the pollen and chaff of the day's labor puckered at the bridge of my nose. I sneezed again.

"My goodness," Peggy said.

"It's the draft"—I sneezed—"from the window you opened. May I close it?"

"No."

"O.K. Kill me." My body tensed with the coming sneeze and, as if wrestling me down, she tightly wrapped her arm around my chest; this minute alteration, her encircling arm, in my chemical condition cleared my senses, which had been drowning.

"So sensitive." Her voice was dry. "You never should have left your mother's womb."

"It was wonderful in there," I admitted. "Perfect room temperature." Her silence led me to ask, "Have you been listening?"

"I couldn't hear. Did you dissect me?"

"What a thing to say."

"I felt you both thought I was being stupid. I don't care. I feel better."

"Good. Don't stop hugging."

"Your legs are like ice. What *did* you talk about?"

"About the farm, mostly. Whether or not I should mow on Sunday. How's your bleeding?"

"Abundant. I think I'm sympathetic with the rain."

"You poor girl. You need a baby."

"I have one. Two, counting Richard."

"Can't I please close the window? My mother thinks I'm coming down with a cold."

"If you must. I'll suffocate."

To close the window I left the bed. The small thump of the sash seemed to trigger the night; lightning flashed behind Schoelkopf's hill, followed by thunder. I got back into bed facing Peggy. Her warmth altered my flesh. She put her oval hand upon me. "My goodness," she said again.

"Think nothing of it," I said. "It's stupid Nature."

"Shall I do anything?"

"Sweetie, no. You work too hard at being a wife. Just relax. Be yourself."

Obediently her hand left me. Beneath and beyond us there was a barking of dogs and an answering banging of doors.

"So you laid for a Yalie," I said. "I'll be damned."

I DREAD DREAMING of my children. When I first left them, it never happened. If I fell asleep at all it was into oblivion. Then, as my separation from Joan acquired its own set of habits and became somewhat usual, it happened every night. I could not close my eyes without Ann or Martha coming to me with wide pale faces, with tangled strings to unknot, broken toys to mend, difficult sentences to explain, impossible puzzles to help them with. After my marriage to Peggy the dreams became less frequent. Tonight's was the first in a week. I was mowing. The tractor stumbled over something; there was a muffled nick. I stopped and dismounted, dreading the discovery of shattered pheasant eggs. The field changed underfoot. I was picking my way through a strange landscape, like a vacant lot, only tufty, like a swamp, and smoldering, like a dump. Something curled up was lying caked with ashen dirt. Abruptly anxious, overswept with pity, I picked it up and examined it and discovered it to be alive. It was a stunted human being, a hunched homunculus, its head sunk on its chest as if shying from a blow. A tiny voice said, "It's me." The face beneath the caked dirt was, though shrunk, familiar. Who was it? "Don't you know me, Daddy? I'm Charlie." I pressed him against my chest and vowed never to be parted from him.

My mother's voice was saying my name. Her face followed, enlarging, bending closer. She was wearing a dark green dress and her hair was down.

I asked, "Are you going to church?"

"I think I better," she said. "I had a poor night."

It was morning. I realized that Charlie was not in my arms, that he existed in Canada as a healthy, firm-bodied boy. I realized that, from my bare shoulders showing above the blanket, my mother would think Peggy and I had slept naked after making love. Peggy was not in the bed.

"I heard dogs barking," I said, trying to agree with a statement I couldn't contradict.

"When there's a wind, the door they put on the barn when they took away the overhang rattles in a way the dogs don't like. Are you going to come with me?"

"To church?"

"It would please your father."

"What about Peggy and Richard?"

"Richard says he didn't bring the right clothes."

"What time is it?"

"Quarter of nine. The service is at nine-thirty this month." The church was half of a split parish; the minister gave each Sunday service twice, at nine-thirty and eleven, at two churches miles apart.

"Where's Peggy?"

"Outdoors in her Iwo Jima. I haven't eaten her."

"Did you ask her to go?"

"She says she'll go if Richard changes his mind."

"What about going by yourself?"

"I don't trust myself with the car, and wouldn't you like to see if there's still people out there who remember you?"

"No."

"To tell the truth I've hardly been all summer and I feel guilty about it."

"Well. I can't get dressed if you keep standing there."

"Would you really mind? It's the last thing like this I'll try to ask of you." And I realized that she had expected me to refuse.

But I wanted to go to church and to see, only see, other people, people unrelated to me except through the strange courtesy, paid the universe, of Christian belief. Like, I suppose, my father, the deacon, I needed to test my own existence against the fact of their faces and clean clothes and hushed shoulders, to regather myself in a vacant hour. The congregation this morning was small. In their accustomed

front pews sat the Henry brothers, all three of them, a feed
merchant and a tractor dealer and a schoolteacher, with their
interchangeably plump wives and some surviving children
(Jessica, Tom Henry's eldest daughter, had moved to Santa Fe
with her pilot husband; Morris, Willis Henry's son, had married a Roman Catholic girl and undergone conversion) and
even a few grandchildren, in laundered shirts and starched
dresses, wriggling and staring. Behind them, after the space
of two empty pews, sat a red-necked blond couple that, my
mother whispered, had opened a luncheonette toward Galilee.
Across the aisle, old Mrs. Rouck, in her timeless black hat
with metal berries, shared a pew with the slim Puerto Rican
grass widow who lived (my mother whispered) in a trailer
parked on the old Gougler place. She sat very erect, a gray
veil enclosing her brown profile, while her children bobbed
up and down beanlike beside her. I did not know any of the
men who took the collection; they were a new type in the
county, junior businessmen in correct single-breasted summer suits, engineers, dentists, commuting clerks. I was re-
lieved to see no one, beyond the Henrys and ancient Katie
Rouck, who might remember me from the days when I, a
sullen sophisticate, came to this church between my parents.
Above the altar, there had been a dim mural of the Ascension,
stained by the smoke of funeral candles, painted by a travel-
ling artist a half-century ago. Christ's feet, peeping from beneath the hem of his robe as He discreetly lifted in flight, had
been utterly relaxed. Now here hung a pleated cardinal dossal
backing a brazen modernist cross, the gift, my mother whispered, of Russell Henry in memory of his parents. The service was perfectly familiar, though years had passed since I
had last heard it. The responses came to my lips inevitably.
The minister, sleek and very young, ten years younger than I,
moved through the forms with a nasal pedantic voice and
practiced gestures; as he crossed to the pulpit he revealed that

he was very short, a fact hidden in the uncertain perspective of the presbytery.

He took as his text Genesis 2:18. The sermon was rotundly enunciated and quaintly learned; his face and nervous hands seemed pale in the upward light of the lectern. *And the Lord God said, It is not good that the man should be alone; I will make him an help meet for him.* Notice, first, that Adam's need was a "help meet." In Hebrew the word is *azer*, meaning, without connotations of sex, "aid," "help" such as an apprentice might render a master, or one laborer another. We were, then, men and women, put here not, as some sentimental theologies would have it, to love one another, but to *work* together. Work is not a consequence of the Fall. When Creation was fresh and unsullied, God set Adam in Eden "to dress it and to keep it." To keep it, the minister repeated.

The next verse reads, *And out of the ground the Lord God formed every beast of the field, and every fowl of the air; and brought them unto Adam to see what he would call them: and whatsoever Adam called every living creature, that was the name thereof.* Two things strike us as curious. One, God—naïvely, it would seem—created the animals, before Eve, as help mates, as companions to Adam in his loneliness! Two, Adam's first piece of work, the first piece of work the Bible describes for us, is to *name* these animals! Are these facts so curious? Are not the dumb creatures of the earth in very truth our companions? Does not some glint of God's original intention shine out from the eyes of the dog, the horse, the heifer even as she is slaughtered? Has not Man, in creating civilization, looked to the animals not only as beasts of burden and sustenance but for inspiration, as in the flight of the birds and the majesty of lions? Has not, in honesty, an eternal pact been honored and kept? And is it so strange that Adam's first piece of work was to name his mute helpers? Is not language an act of husbandry, a fencing-in of fields? All of us here are farmers or the sons and daughters of farmers, so we know how the lowly earthworm aërates the soil. Likewise, language aërates the barren density of brute matter with the penetrations of the mind, of the spirit.

I whispered to my mother, "I wasn't the son of a farmer."

"Shh. You're my son too."

And the Lord God caused a deep sleep to fall upon Adam, and he slept: and he took one of his ribs, and closed up the flesh instead; and the rib, which the Lord God had taken from man, made he a woman, and brought her unto the man. As some of you doubtlessly know, this passage was cited to justify the first use of ether in operations, when it was feared that anesthesia might be unchristian. But let us direct our attention to three other features of Eve's creation. She was taken *out of* Adam. She was made *after* Adam. And she was made while Adam slept. What do these assertions tell us about men and women today? First, is not Woman's problem that she was taken *out of* Man, and is therefore a subspecies, less than equal to Man, a part of the world? The term Mankind includes Womankind and on the chess board the Queen, though supremely powerful, is numbered among the "men." Webster defines *woman* as "an adult female person, as distinguished from a man or a child." The impression lingers that, so distinguished, she lies somewhere between, as the philosopher Schopenhauer observed.

The Henry brothers looked at each other and there was polite laughter from the front pews.

Second, she was made *after* Man. Think of God as a workman who learns as he goes. Man is the rougher and stronger artifact; Woman the finer and more efficient. She was fashioned, observe, soon after God had "formed every beast of the field, and every fowl of the air" and his hand, still turning to those same rhythms, imparted to Woman a creaturely shapeliness. A rib is rounded. Man, with Woman's creation, became confused as to where to turn. With one half of his being he turns toward her, his rib, as if into himself, into the visceral warmth wherein his tensions find *re*solution in *dis*solution. With his other half of his being he gazes outward, toward God, along the straight line of infinity. He seeks to *solve* the riddle of his death. Eve does not. In a sense she does not know death. Her very name, *Hava*, means "living." Her motherhood answers concretely what men would answer abstractly. But we as Christians all know that there is no abstract answer, that there is no answer whatsoever apart from the concrete reality of Christ.

His sharp face grew paler, leaning into the light of the lectern.

And third, Woman was made while Adam slept. Her beauty will ever have in men's eyes a dreamlike quality. Each day we men awake like Adam puzzled to find ourselves duplicated—no, not duplicated, for the expectant softness and graceful patience of the other stand in strange contrast to us. In reaching out to her, Adam commits an act of faith.

And Adam said, This is now bone of my bone, and flesh of my flesh; she shall be called Woman, because she was taken out of Man. The original language of Genesis has grammatical gender. Man, *ish*, calls Woman *isha*—signifies her, that is, as an aspect of himself. A necessary aspect. Karl Barth, the great theologian of the Reformed Church, our partner in the Reformation, says this of Woman: "Successfully or otherwise, she is in her whole existence an appeal to the kindness of Man." An appeal to the kindness of Man. "For kindness," he goes on to say, "belongs originally to his particular responsibility as a man." Belongs *originally*: since the beginning, since God breathed life into the nostrils of the dust and "man became a living soul."

So Woman, if I have not misunderstood these verses, was put on earth to help Man do his work, which is God's work. She is less than Man, and superior to him. In designating her with his own generic name, Adam commits an act of faith: "This is *now* bone of my bones, and flesh of my flesh." In so declaring, he acknowledges within himself a responsibility to be kind. He ties himself ethically to the earth. Kindness differs from righteousness as the grasses from the stars. Both are infinite. Without conscious confession of God, there can be no righteousness. But kindness needs no belief. It is implicit in the nature of Creation, in the very curves and amplitude of God's perfect fashioning. Let us pray.

At the door, taking the minister's limp and chill little hand, I told him, avoiding his black bold eyes—very local eyes— that his sermon had been excellent.

Behind me in the line, my mother in turn told him, in the level low tone with which she expresses reservations, "It's so unusual to hear a *young* sermon."

In the car, I asked her, "Why did the sermon seem young?"

"Oh I don't know," she said. "I get so tired of men talking about women. Women just aren't that interesting to me."

"I thought he was bright."

"Oh, he'll go places. This parish won't hold him much longer. He'll be a bishop by forty if his eyes don't rove."

I laughed. "Do his eyes rove?"

"There's been talk. We have some very pretty women in the choir now." The sermon nagged her, for after a silence she said, "No, Joey, it seems to me whenever a man begins to talk that way, he's trying to excuse himself from some woman's pain."

Her tone surprised me, it arose so purely from within. My mother's inner weather had an egocentric independence of me that I disliked. I changed the subject. "Do the Henrys know about my divorce?" We had talked with them briefly after church, in the shadowless mid-morning heat, standing on the reddish stones and packed dirt of the parking area. They were cordial and courteous to me, and I asked after Jessica, whose smooth limbs and wide-set gray eyes I had once

admired so keenly my country bed had complained. Russell
and Willis and Tom all called my mother by her first name,
Mary, which took us, standing before this old-time church
with the keystone dated 1882 and a milk-glass fanlight above
the front portal, back into a time when I did not exist. They
had been schoolchildren together. I felt it had tired my mother,
slipping back into such an older self.

"Oh sure," she answered. "There was a good deal of interest around here. We're keeping an eye on you." Her voice
sounded tight and seemed held far forward in her body.

"I'm sorry. Was everybody shocked?"

"It takes a lot to shock us now. Last winter the mayor of Alton was indicted for taking kickbacks from the naughty places
up by the fairgrounds."

I laughed again; there has never been anybody for making
me laugh like my mother. "Still, I don't want to be a local
scandal. You have to live your life here."

"Oh, Joey, I think you think we're all foolish back here.
They met Joan. They could see she wasn't right for you."

"Wasn't she right?" I felt, steering the car down the road, in
a precarious place; I felt a blessing trying, very delicately, to
break through to me.

My mother's voice was impatient. "Of course not. This one's
more your style. The Hofstetters always had high-stepping
women."

This was too harsh, dismissed too lightly my first, my ten-
der and deep, my silent and inward wife. Joan was sealed in
me like an illusion too painful to disavow.

"Well," I said, "we don't want to disappoint the Hofstetters."

"You know what I mean. Blood must flow. You have a
streak of your father in you, you tend to be too obliging. You
were becoming something very tame before I brought us to
the farm. That's why I did it. That's what you went back to
when you married Joan. Joan was like Olinger. Respectable.
Ni-ice."

Her sneered pronunciation hurt me. "Now Mother, you're just talking. And you're running out of breath."

"That isn't all I'm running out of."

"What's the matter?"

There was a strange quality to her pauses, an unspoken re-gathering after each utterance. "Just keep your eye on the road. Your job, for instance. I never forgave Joan for letting you waste yourself on that ridiculous job. Consulting!"

"She never told me not to quit."

"That wasn't enough. It was her place to *tell* you to quit. She never got out from behind those proud blue eyes to look at you, Joey."

"That's not true." But I felt my pulse racing and a selfish joy lifting from this smothered combat. My mother screamed. It was not a full scream but a prolonged whimper such as a dog emits when its forepaws are squeezed. I was making the left turn off the highway onto our road, so a second or two passed before I dared turn my head to look at her. It was she yet not she. Her face, especially about the eye sockets, was swollen, as if straining to contain an impact delivered from within; she folded her fat arms across her chest and, eyelids lowered, bore down. The planes of her face, like those of a cloud, eluded perspective. The space between her eyebrows was damp.

"What shall I do?"

"Keep going. I've had these before."

"That was a frightening noise you made."

This criticism seemed to catch her as she was about to make another, for her lips clamped upon a quick high grunt, and in silence her face surrendered to that terrible infusion of fullness, which smoothed her wrinkles away.

"My God, Mother!"

Now, a wave having broken, she breathed, eyes still closed, in sharp shallow gasps that parted her lips, as if alert to be kissed. I took my foot from the accelerator and moved it to the brake. She opened her eyes; they were merciless, expressionless. "Don't stop. Get me onto my land."

"Well that's silly, if you need a doctor."

She said quickly. "My pills are there." She seemed to listen, to judge she had time for a playful apology. "There's been too much excitement these last two days. I lead a quiet life."

I let the car get moving again. The smaller field, still shaggy, skimmed by us. The sweep of the field I had mowed came into view. As we passed the pear tree, she screamed again, a louder but lower noise, almost a moan. I felt flattered that she permitted herself this outcry, having suppressed, out of respect for my innocence, the first two.

"Is it in the heart?" I asked.

She answered, "The arms and the chest muscles more. I suppose when it reaches the heart I won't be here to tell it." I drove in across the lawn and stopped by the back porch. The dogs barked but otherwise the place seemed deserted; the pump and the split privet bush looked like trespassers frozen by fright at our appearance.

"Can you walk?"

"I think so, but I can't open the door."

I thought she meant that the handle of the Citroën was strange to her. Then I saw that she was making no attempt to move her arms. I went around and let her out. She permitted me to touch her, to put my hand under her elbow. Though her feet seemed firm on the grass, she remained hunched and hesitated before stepping away from the support of the car. "The dogs will need a run," she said. Their yapping was frantic; perhaps for them our conjunction formed a new creature worrisomely compounded of smells and outlines they trusted. As we slowly moved around the front of the car, the puppy upset the dry water pan and one of the adult dogs, in leaping and falling, raked the wire mesh with his claws.

No one was in the house. The breakfast dishes, which we

had been too hurried to clear from the table, were soaking in steel-colored water from which the suds had evaporated. The silently running electric clock, the glistening presents I had sent from far cities, the preoccupied photographs continued their vigil uninterrupted. We were ghosts from a sphere that never impinged upon theirs.

"Peggy? Peggy! Richard!"

There was no answer. My mother said, "Let me go now, Joey. I'll go upstairs and lie down. Thank you for taking me to church."

"Can you make it by yourself?"

"If I don't, you'll hear me fall."

And this was how, with our old-fashioned mutual courtesy and fear of touching one another, we managed. She went up alone, her right arm lifted enough to keep her hat in place, while I waited below until her shuffling footsteps crossed diagonally above me. I called out, "O.K.?"

Her answer, which I hardly heard, seemed to be, "Never better!"

I shouted, "I'll go find Peggy!" Would my mother take this as a desertion? I meant it to be a rescue. That I myself could not rescue her had become suddenly clear. As I ran across the lawn my stomach grovelled with that conviction, remembered from childhood, of unworthiness, of guilt, of the world being an important, gala parade that I had somehow missed and that, as I raced through the darkening streets of Olinger, I could dimly overhear but could not find.

I did not know which way to run. Weeds thrust everywhere; the malevolent idleness of Sunday lay on everything. The farm seemed no longer a lush and fabled haven remote from the highways but a wild place fifteen minutes from Alton, an unpoliced emptiness attracting slumdwellers, a vacuum pulling into itself madmen and rapists. My son—for it was as such that Richard figured in the mental shorthand of panic—

was in my mind as a pitiable witness, more pitied by me, more clearly pictured in his helpless bright-eyed onlooking, than his mother, my wife, the actual victim, the mangled nude. I ran to the mailbox and looked down the road. It was empty, making a thin S in its retreat up the rise to Schoelkopf's mailbox. Above it hung the reddish dust of a car's recent passing. I turned toward the great field and prepared to run into it when behind me a voice found my name.

"Joey!"

It was Richard, coming out from behind the barn. He had been hidden by the blind curve. He was wearing his new sunglasses and his face without his eyes looked pale and uncertain, a little hippy's, his mouth miniature and sarcastic. He turned and shouted into the air, "It's them!"

"Where's your mother?"

"Picking blackberries." As we trotted down the road to the tobacco shed foundation, he told me, "A car went by full of men and we crouched down in the bushes." The heavy sky was here and there wearing thin, so that colorless small shadows bounced at our feet.

Peggy, bare-shouldered in her bikini, was up to her hips in brambles, serenely reaching toward those thickest and best berries closest to the sun-crumbled stucco of the old wall. She seemed a doe of my species, grazing immune in a thicket. My impression of her beloved body immersed in thorns was qualified by the discovery that, though she wore above her waist only the little polka-dot bra, her bottom half was sheathed in the blue stretch pants that imitated dungarees; in this centaurine costume she seemed more naturally, more practically resolved to give herself—my city wife, my habituée of foyers and automatic elevators—to the farm. "I did a very stupid thing," she told me. "A car went by a while ago with a lot of sinister men and I hid in what I think must be poison ivy."

"The leaves go in threes and are shiny."

She looked down. "Oh God, yes. It'll be all over my belly."

"You can use the yellow soap again. You better come up to the house anyway. My mother's had some kind of an attack."

"Joey, no. How bad?"

"I can't tell. Maybe you can tell."

Richard asked me, "Have you telephoned the police for the ambulance yet?"

I told him, "I wouldn't know who to call. I have no idea how you get an ambulance out here."

Peggy said, "Stop scaring yourselves." Yet as she said it, her face, small amid her loose tangled hair, showed enough fright to keep her one of us. With care she removed her body from the brambles, holding high a colander half-full of berries. Richard hurried ahead up the road; I knew how he felt. There was a parade he was afraid of missing and afraid of catching. Peggy walked beside me and without breaking stride submitted to my caress when, hidden from the eyes of the house by the barn, I touched first the damp base of her neck and followed her spine with my fingers and went beyond to where the curve curved under into the crotch of her pants. I felt this long living line as a description of love stretched thin—as in those new paintings whose artists, returning to nature from the realm of abstraction, render a sky an impossible earth-red which nevertheless answers to our eyes as sky.

PEGGY WENT UP to my mother, was with her a time, and came down saying she was in bed and seemed subdued but amiable. She had taken her pills and gotten into bed and the sense of suffocation was diminishing, though the pain in her arm was spreading to her entire left side. She and Peggy had agreed I should call the doctor, though he was probably at church. He was a Mennonite. Peggy sent Richard upstairs with the blackberries, and I went to the phone, which sat on the sill of the window that looked toward the barn. There was a quarter-column of Graafs in the phone book but only one doctor. His phone didn't answer. While listening to it ring, I studied the barn, whose appearance, without the ungainly overhang, had something dreadful about it, and it came to me that the barn had been my parents, and my father was gone. Where the overhang had been I could look through to a piece of meadow and a stand of sumac with a few leaves prematurely turned red, as if individually poisoned. The phone didn't answer. Above me, Richard laughed, and my mother's voice musically picked its way along the edge of some flirting assertion. Peggy, brushing her hair back from her face, set about making lunch. The dogs were barking.

I went outside and took their leashes, with the augmenting lengths of clothesline, from the nail on the porch post, where they hung near the measuring cup we drank from. I went into the pen and as the dogs leaped and swivelled around me clipped the leashes to their collars. The puppy could run free. The two bigger dogs, noses down, ears flattened, pulled me through the orchard. Their shoulder fur was fluffed with the joy of being out and when they pulled against their collars too hard they hacked and coughed. My hand, wrapped around with rope, burned with pressure; along the row of sunflowers they caught a scent and pulled so hard I had to run or let go. In the garden, the low-spreading dark leaves of the strawberry rows were being smothered by the taller growths of milkweed, burdock, and plantain. The earth Peggy had turned had faded and reconstituted its crust. The tugging dogs, all eager muscle, pulled me across the road to the fascinating new world, bared spoor and burrows, of the field I had mowed.

Drying stripes of dead grass diagrammed the pattern I had pursued. The stubble was dotted, in abundance, with flowers that had evaded the cutter or had been born yesterday; *flowers*, I thought, *the first advertisements*, and wondered if I could use the thought in my work. The puppy startled a butterfly into two butterflies, itself and its shadow.

Our shadows had a noontide smallness. Shapelessly being burned away, the clouds had the persistence of a dull ache, and collectively seemed a ruined strategy, a confusedly ebbing life. I wanted to return and feared the dogs would drag me to the end of the farm. But when, just beyond the crown of the big field, from which the silver tip of the Alton courthouse could be glimpsed in winter, I brought them to a halt, they obediently turned and, as if picking up the scent of the homeward leg of my mother's routine walks with them, took me along the hedgerow of sumac and ailanthus, and along the lower edge of the field, past the tobacco shed foundation, across the road, and into our yard. Bustling happily, pretending to resist, they submitted to the pen. The skirts of fur at their hind legs were loaded with burs and the small green seeds shaped like rounded arrowheads. I looked down and saw that nature had also used me; the cuffs of my trousers were also seed-bearing.

Inside the house, Richard was reading and Peggy, having made sandwiches of Lebanon balony, was heating mushroom soup. The table was set for three. "How is she?"

Richard said, "She said the blackberries were very good and she didn't want any lunch." The book he was reading was my Wodehouse novel.

Peggy asked, "Do you want to try the doctor again before we eat?"

"Are you sure she wants the doctor?"

"She said so. Why wouldn't she?"

"It seems unlike her."

Peggy's eyes, watching her hands pour milk, lifted. Her glance was offended; I remembered my mother's unexpected remark about men excusing themselves from women's pain. "Go up and ask her," Peggy said.

Climbing the stairs, still in my suit, I felt a stiffness in my side coat pocket and pulled out the folded church program. It had been my father's habit to fold the program and stick it in his pocket rather than throw it away. He had been reluctant to throw anything away, an ineffectual tenderness that had exasperated me as a boy. I laid the obsolete program on the stack of magazines that still awaited disposal on the window-sill at the head of the stairs.

"Mother?"

She was asleep, half-propped up on two pillows, one bare arm lying on top of the blanket. Her hair, seen from above, seemed entirely white, and her hand, lying palm-up beside the colander of berries—Peggy had picked too many green—had the loose-clenched chunkiness of a child's. Sleep deepened the lines running from the wings of her nose to the corners of her mouth and had drawn parallel secondary creases down through the flesh of her cheeks, where no wrinkles had been before. I saw her, now, as an old woman. Always before she had appeared to me as a heavier version of the swift young mother outsprinting my father from the barn. I had felt this woman within her and had felt that she was withheld from me as a punishment. In sleep my mother had slipped from my recognition and blame and had entered, unconsciously, a far territory, the arctic of the old. The underside of her curiously smooth arm was silvery in the light that at the window strained gold from the wilt-rimmed leaves of the geraniums standing potted on the sill. I realized that my mother must water and tend and "keep" these plants, in this room where she said she never slept, and I felt all around me, throughout the farm, a thousand such details of nurture about to sink into the earth with her. Death seemed something minor, a defect she had overlooked in purchasing these acres, a negligible flaw grown huge. She made a tranquil snoring noise; her limp hand fidgeted; I removed the quarter-full colander from the danger of spilling. I bent over my mother's form as once on a beach I had examined the wobbly outline my children had traced around my body as I lay stretched on the sand. My shape had seemed grotesquely small, emptied of life's vibrations.

I went into our bedroom and changed out of my suit. Downstairs, Peggy, seeing me again in my father's dungarees, asked, "Are you going to mow?"

"I can't, it's Sunday."

"Are we going back today, or what?"

"I don't know if we can."

"*Please* call the doctor."

"I'm scared to."

"Don't be such a baby."

This time someone answered, Doc Graaf's wife. Her tone suggested she had been taken from the Sunday dinner table. She called my news into the next room and relayed to me the doctor's answer. He would come at two-thirty. In the meantime I should let my mother sleep.

We ate lunch. Richard asked when we were going home.

"Do you want to go home? I thought you liked the farm."

"There's nothing to do here."

"My mother would be very sad to hear you say that."

"She did. I told her and she agreed. She said she liked it here because she had never been a doer."

"We can't go home until we know how sick she is. I may have to send you and *your* mother home alone." In anticipation of full ownership, my heart expanded to the limits, the far corners and boundary-stones, of the farm. Soon it would be fall, the trees transparent, the sky clean, the stars pressing at night, asters everywhere, first frost.

Peggy said, "I think she needs a trained nurse staying with her."

I said, "Maybe we could get Joan to do it. She needs a job. Then I could pay her her alimony as a salary."

"Is that supposed to be funny?"

"Do you know what trained nurses *cost*?"

"A lot less than *I* cost, is I suppose what you're saying."

"A hell of a lot less. But that's still plenty."

Richard said, "We could call her every night at some appointed hour to see if she's all right."

I said to him, "Maybe we could get a private television circuit so we could watch her whenever we turned the switch."

"I read somewhere where they already have those in baby wards in hospitals."

"Excuse me. Behind the times again."

Peggy said, "Don't pick on Richard. You can take your foul temper out on me but not on him."

"Oh? I thought we were all legally one. You and me and Richard and Dean McCabe and four dozen other gentlemen not specifically identified."

She reached across the table and tried to slap me; I caught her wrist in mid-air and twisted it so she had to sit down again. The exchange, transpiring in Richard's wide eyes, perversely worked to her advantage. Though for a second my animus had surfaced, her decent simplicity washed over me again, around me, under me. Holding the wrist I had hurt in her other hand, she enunciated, "One thing I want very clear with you, Joey. Don't throw Joan in my face like that again. You made your choice. I had no power over you and tried to be honest with you and you made your choice. If you have anything constructive to say to me say it, but don't tease me like you did that dog. Don't keep showing me the hole. If I have to make any sacrifices so your mother gets proper care of course I'll make them, but I'm not Joan and we all knew it at the time and I'm not going to act sorry."

I attempted to apologize, for I knew it was by accident that she had come between me and my momentary vision of the farm, the farm as mine, in the fall, the warmth of its leaves and the retreat of its fields and the benign infinity of its twigs. I said, "Don't be dumb. You're great." But my failure to be able to cherish both her and the farm at once seemed somehow a failure of hers, a rigidity that I lived with in virtual silence until at two-thirty promptly the doctor came, smelling of antiseptic soap and sauerkraut.

WHEN THE DOCTOR had gone, we went upstairs. Richard and Peggy kept their distance from the bed, while I went closer. It was after three o'clock and I could feel the Sunday evening traffic building on the Turnpike. My mother was propped up in bed, her gray hair dark against the white pillow. She seemed slimmer; her skin had the papery look of the recently awakened and her slightly twisted lips seemed amused. "What did he say to *you*?"

"He said we should consider your going to a hospital."

"For how long?"

"Until the likelihood of these attacks lessens."

"Why would the likelihood lessen? Why doesn't he want me to die here where I belong? My parents died here, my husband died here, I want to die *here*. It seems little enough to ask from these medical buzzards. All these drugs, just to prolong your misery. I'm not leaving my land."

"It's not a question of your dying. It's a question of your comfort and your getting better."

"You know better than that." She gazed at me directly; her eyes were very clear. They had simply ceased to ask for anything other than the truth. At thirty-five, I felt still too young to live in this element. Tempering herself to me, or lapsing into old habits, she began to clown, to exaggerate. "The ghost in me wants to get out. I can feel it pushing."

I fell in with her tone. "You know," I said, "you mustn't think only of yourself. You must think of how it makes me look. From the way Doc Graaf shook hands good-bye, I don't think he thinks I'm much of a son."

"Oh," she said, "the Hofstetters never did have much of a name in this township, it's too late to worry about the neighbors now. We've always been cranks and villains. They liked your father, because he came from out-of-state and made them feel superior, but you and me—we're beyond help, Joey."

"Please don't let the money be a factor." Through this she could see that I would let her have her way, and could know that I was grateful for her insisting on what I could not propose.

Her arm lifted impatiently. "When isn't money a factor? Of course it's a factor. Isn't it, Peggy?"

Peggy came forward a step. "Would you like us to stay?"

"Thank you, Peggy, but I want you to go. I want you all to go back to New York where you belong. You've done your duty, all three of you, and you've made this old woman very happy, and it's not your fault her arteries couldn't take so much happiness."

Peggy said, "But we can't leave you helpless in bed."

"Who says I'm helpless? I'll get up when I have to. The Schoelkopfs keep an eye on my chimney and when no smoke shows they'll come over. The dogs will bark. Isn't there a saying about lying in the bed you've made?" She patted the blanket. "Well if ever a woman made her bed, I'm the one." There was in her small laugh the vanity she must have had as a young woman, and that had hardened into a tricky pride by the time I knew her.

She looked at Richard. "Will you come again, Richard?"

Unsmiling, he nodded, his brown eyes fascinated and embarrassed and bright.

"The next time," she promised, "I'll try not to get between you and your mother. That's a naughty thing for an old witch to do."

"We can wait until dark," I said suddenly, almost exclaiming, for my nerves had become taut, pulling me back toward the city, away from this sickness. "I should mow some more."

My mother's squarish hand, short-fingered and worn like a man's, dismissed the offer indisputably. "Don't worry about the mowing, Joey," she said. "Sammy can finish it up some day. You did the man-sized part." She turned her head and said to Peggy, "He's a good boy and I've always been tempted to overwork him."

"He *is* a good boy." Affirming this, Peggy grinned, grinned at me as in my dream of her in the farmhouse window or as she had the first time we met, at a party in an apartment whose large abstract paintings seemed windows overlooking a holocaust. I felt lost here—idle, unconsulted; my life felt misplaced. She had been standing talking to Joan; at my approach the two women, Joan in blue and Peggy in wheat-yellow, had turned to face me, and when Joan said, *This is my husband*, Peggy's hand stabbed mannishly toward mine and she grinned with startling width, as if incredulous.

"That's the smile," my mother said. "Peggy. The next time you come, if you can stand it and I'm still alive, I'd like you to go have your picture taken for me."

New York, the city that is always its own photograph, the living memento of my childish dream of escape, called to me, urged me away, into the car, down the road, along the highway, up the Turnpike. I was ashamed of my desire yet confirmed in it. My mother turned once more to me; her eyes were young with tears not quite free of pleading.

"Joey," she said, "when you sell my farm, don't sell it cheap. Get a good price."

We were striking terms, and circumspection was needed. I must answer in our old language, our only language, allusive and teasing, that with conspiratorial tact declared nothing and left the past apparently unrevised.

"*Your* farm?" I said. "I've always thought of it as our farm."

read more Ⓟ

PENGUIN MODERN CLASSICS

RABBIT, RUN
JOHN UPDIKE

'Brilliant and poignant ... By his compassion, clarity of insight, and crystal-bright prose, [Updike] makes Rabbit's sorrow his and our own' *Washington Post*

It's 1959 and Harry 'Rabbit' Angstrom, one time high school sports superstar, is going nowhere. At twenty-six he is trapped in a second-rate existence – stuck with a fragile, alcoholic wife, a house full of overflowing ashtrays and discarded glasses, a young son and a futile job. With no way to fix things, he resolves to flee from his family and his home in Pennsylvania, beginning a thousand-mile journey that he hopes will free him from his mediocre life. Because, as he knows only too well, 'after you've been first-rate at something, no matter what, it kind of takes the kick out of being second-rate.'

'Updike's punch is powerful' *Newsweek*

PENGUIN MODERN CLASSICS

RABBIT IS RICH
JOHN UPDIKE

'The power of the novel comes from a sense, not absolutely unworthy of Thomas Hardy, that the universe hangs over our fates like a great sullen hopeless sky. There is real pain in the book, and a touch of awe' Norman Mailer, *Esquire*

It's 1979 and Rabbit is no longer running. He's walking, and beginning to get out of breath. That's OK, though – it gives him the chance to enjoy the wealth that comes with middle age. It's all in place: he's Chief Sales Representative and co-owner of Springer motors; his wife, at home or in the club, is keeping trim; he wears good suits, and the cash is pouring in. So why is it that he finds it so hard to accept the way that things have turned out? And why, when he looks at his family, is he haunted by regrets about all those lives he'll never live?

With an afterword by John Updike

Winner of the 1982 Pulitzer Prize for Fiction

PENGUIN MODERN CLASSICS

RABBIT REDUX
JOHN UPDIKE

'A superb performance, all grace and dazzle...a brilliant portrait of middle America' *Life*

It's 1969, and the times are changing. America is about to land a man on the moon, the Vietnamese war is in full swing, and racial tension is on the rise. Things just aren't as simple as they used to be – at least, not for Rabbit Angstrom. His wife has left him with his teenage son, his job is under threat and his mother is dying. Suddenly, into his confused life – and home – comes Jill, an eighteen-year-old runaway who becomes his lover. But when she invites her friend to stay, a young black radical named Skeeter, the pair's fragile harmony soon begins to fail …

'Updike owns a rare verbal genius, a gifted intelligence and a sense of tragedy made bearable by wit. A masterpiece' *Time*

With an afterword by John Updike

Penguin Modern Classics

RABBIT AT REST
JOHN UPDIKE

'Among prose works which address the American century, Rabbit has few obvious betters ... this novel is endutingly eloquent about weariness, age and disgust, in a prose that is always fresh, nubile and witherable' Martin Amis

It's 1989, and Harry 'Rabbit' Angstrom is far from restful. Fifty-six and overweight, he has a struggling business on his hands and a heart that is starting to fail. His family, too, are giving him cause for concern. His son Nelson is a wreck of a man, a cocaine addict with shattered self-respect. Janice, his wife, has decided that she wants to be a working girl. And as for Pru, his daughter-in-law, she seems to be sending out signals to Rabbit that he knows he should ignore, but somehow can't. He has to make the most of life, after all. He doesn't have much time left ...

'One of the finest literary achievements to have come out of the US since the war. Rabbit may well be that much haunted and, so we thought, mythical beast: the Great American novel' John Banville

With a new afterword by Justin Cartwright

read more ⟨Penguin⟩

PENGUIN MODERN CLASSICS

ROGER'S VERSION
JOHN UPDIKE

'At once generously realist, wickedly surrealist and fabulous, in the great
American Tradition' A. S. Byatt

A born-again computer whiz kid bent on proving the existence of God on his
computer meets a middle-aged divinity professor, Roger Lambert, who'd just as
soon leave faith a mystery. Soon the computer hacker begins an affair with
Professor Lambert's wife – and Roger finds himself experiencing deep longings
for a trashy teenage girl ...

'Exalted and demonic, heartless and sentimental, magnanimous and mean...
a tremendously expert novel' Martin Amis

With a new afterword by John Banville

PENGUIN MODERN CLASSICS

THE POORHOUSE FAIR
JOHN UPDIKE

'A work of art' *The New York Times*

Published just four years after John Updike graduated from Harvard, *The Poorhouse Fair* is a brilliant allegory about charity. The setting is a poorhouse – repository of the old, the infirm, and the impoverished – on the day of the annual summer fair. The people are the vividly realized, unforgettable characters that only Updike can create. Short and succinct, *The Poorhouse Fair* speaks to those fears all of us have of growing not old, but dependent.

'A first novel of rare precision and real merit ... A rich poorhouse indeed'
Newsweek

With a new afterword by John Updike

PENGUIN MODERN CLASSICS

THE COMPLETE HERNY BECH
JOHN UPDIKE

'One of Updike's best creations' *Life*

Bech: A Book; *Bech is Back*; *Bech in Czech* are here collected in one volume.
A perfect forum for Updike's limber prose, *The Complete Henry Bech* is an arch
portrait of the literary life in America from an incomparable American writer.

'The funniest, most elegantly written and intelligently sympathetic rendition
available about what happens when a writer stops being a writer and becomes a
culture object' *Time*

With an afterword by John Updike